HALLO
TUR

PAUL C. WALSH

G000146583

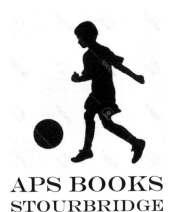

APS BOOKS
STOURBRIDGE

APS Books,
4 Oakleigh Road,
Stourbridge,
West Midlands,
DY8 2JX

APS Books is a subsidiary of
the APS Publications imprint

www.andrewsparke.com

Copyright ©2020 Paul C. Walsh
All rights reserved.

Paul C. Walsh has asserted his right to be identified as the author of this work in accordance with the Copyright Designs and Patents Act 1988

First published worldwide by APS Books in 2020

No part of this publication may be reproduced, stored in or introduced into a retrieval system, or transmitted, in any form, or by any means (electronic, mechanical, photocopying, recording or otherwise) without the written permission of the publisher except that brief selections may be quoted or copied without permission, provided that full credit is given.

ISBN 9781789961256

HALLOWED TURF

Post-match blues

Gerard knew it was a bad idea. Logging on to his *twitter* feed at this hour. It was far too soon. The vitriolic trolls would be at their worst. After all, the dust was still settling from the drama of that afternoon's game. The referee's whistle had blown for full time, barely two hours before. His whistle. It had been a controversial encounter. The stakes were high. Two teams desperate for the points. One of them trying to maintain a challenge for promotion; the other clinging on at the other end of the table, with the spectre of relegation looming ever closer. A match where lots of key decisions would need to be made. By him. Whether it had entailed awarding free kicks for fouls and time wasting, dishing out yellow cards for reckless challenges, or confirming off-side rulings, he felt that he'd called most of them correctly. His assessor had hinted as much. The final outcome: a 2-2 draw. "Something positive for both teams to take from the game," he thought.

Not according to the baying mob at the stadium who screeched in convulsed anger! The two late penalty appeals he turned down for the home side had understandably incensed these fans.

Gerard had always felt uncomfortable about giving penalties. He argued that there were too many players diving around the pitch in an attempt to fool the officials. It was cheating and it was a feature of the modern game he hated. He was also aware that he had a reputation for rarely giving spot kicks. Who knows, on another day, he might have given one, or even both. This was the nub of his defence. Today he was unimpressed with either claim. Those screaming calls from the banks of *town* supporters behind the left goal failed to alter his decision. A nonchalant shake of the head was all it took. Some of these critics would already be vilifying him on social media; attempting to dismantle what was left of his reputation. But he felt safe now, behind the security of his own front door.

Gerard had been advised by several referees he knew to pull his twitter account but had chosen to ignore their advice. After all, there were always the unexpected positive comment to enjoy. That's what others loved about Gerard: his eternal optimism! For that reason, and a morbid fascination with what his detractors had to say, he continued to absorb their hostile feedback. There was no denying that these venomous comments were always more numerous. Compliments appeared very sporadically.

He glanced at his inbox. "Wanker!" "You cheating bastard!" "You gormless twat!" "Your mother is a whore" and more. The usual deranged outbursts from the unbalanced and the obsessed. He had learned to treat such rants with the contempt they deserved. The ramblings of insensitive idiots did not unduly concern him.

But some comments really made his blood boil. Those that drew attention to his name. This riled him because he couldn't do much about it. It was all so puerile and embarrassing. Even if his surname was Pratt.

***

Gerry switched off his computer and headed to the kitchen. A cup of tea and chocolate biscuit might distract him. Sipping his drink, he tried to shut out the subject of names. Names like his. It didn't work. All that pent-up angst resurfaced again in his head, like a wound that refused to heal.

"Ignore it Gerry! You know how it always riles you," his wife Amy had pleaded, not for the first time.

The folly of parents

Later that evening, after Amy had retired to bed to lose herself in her new novel, Gerard's mind returned to the subject that was never far from his thoughts. Why on earth parents were still allowed free reign when it came to naming their children. Parents like his.

Familiar words. Awkward names. The government should impose guidelines!

After all, the opportunity to name a new human being was such a privilege. Surely, there should be some basic advice to help adults in this task. Why? To limit the potential life-changing damage that could unfurl and stop them making the sort of choices that would condemn their off-spring to years of embarrassment and ridicule.

He realised he was talking to himself again.

However, from what he'd seen, common sense has never been mandatory in the ritual of child naming. Instead, ordinarily, sensible adults plunged into imaginings; allowing their thoughts to run wild in the pursuit of new-fangled names; attention grabbing labels for others to identify their offspring by. Gerry had not forgiven his own mum and dad for inflicting this on him. He had noted, enviously, how some people carried their name around like a badge of honour. His conclusion: if you were lucky enough to have the right kind of unusual first name or surname, it could promote curiosity from others or a sense of admiration for such an innovative choice. But if that wasn't true?

His name was certainly not like that. It had come to define him, nevertheless. He'd come close to changing it by deed poll, but his parents would have disowned him. Instead, he stuck with the outcome of his personal naming lottery, acutely embarrassing though it was.

Should those afflicted with names that carried a double meaning, or rude connotations, attempt to hide them away as frequently as possible?

Absolutely, he concluded. Damage limitation. Protect yourself from the vultures itching to pick away at what's left of your self- esteem.

Unfortunately for *Pratt Junior* and with reasons best known to his father, entering this world with a surname that was already bursting with comic potential was not challenging enough. Gerard would concede that he wasn't alone there. There were lots of families identified by similar names to his: well-known, and less than complimentary. In such a situation, he surmised that parents needed to be extremely careful about how they pre-loaded their surnames with first names. In fairness, his mum and dad's decision to call him *Gerard* or *Gerry,* as he preferred to be known, seemed to have alleviated some of the potential for comic ridicule. *Gerard* was a safe choice. *Gerry* even better. It got him off to a reasonable start in a conversation.

But then there was the matter of his middle name. There was another opportunity for a safe choice. With his mother from an Irish Catholic family, one of the Christian saint's names would surely have done. Christopher would have suited nicely, he thought. He liked the popular image of sturdy St. Christopher carrying Jesus on his shoulders across the river. Much more appealing than those other Christian heroes regularly depicted in poses of piety and prayer. His pal, Kevin, had received a safe apostles name. Peter. Good solid name. Another friend, Phil, had entered the world as Philip John. Another harmless choice. Why couldn't Gerard's father do the same? But he had other ideas. What's more, he had form on this topic. He'd already been to the courts to change his own surname after six months of fruitless job applications when he arrived in the country.

His real name was *Yosef Prathar.*

He couldn't mask his Turkish identify but he could do something to sound more British on paper. 'Shorten it to Pratt' his mother had suggested. Yosef was reluctant to comply at first but once he'd done the deed the job interviews started to arrive. He even began calling himself 'Joe' a nickname he'd picked up at one of his jobs.

Employment now secured, he started to enjoy his English name. So much so that he didn't stop there. Mum had always liked her maiden name: *Eymer*. Somewhat unusual for the UK, some might say. One might speculate that such a name was touching on the creative! *Eymer* had dominated the other side of his mother's genealogy tree. Something to do with Staffordshire shoemakers in the late nineteenth century, she had proudly informed him.

But Gerard already had a family name. He was now a *Pratt*. This clearly presented a problem to his father. Apparently oblivious to the dangers attached to such a precarious label, and with a dubious logic accepted by Mrs. Pratt, his parents decided to turn it into a middle name for his son. Gerry, their only child, would proudly carry one of the old names. Not his, but hers. After all, expediency had forced Josef to reluctantly given up his surname. Even more reason that Mum's family link should survive. All that history!

Gerard learned that it would have made little difference if he'd been born a girl. His father had shared with him that they would have seized the chance to call a daughter by the Irish version of this name, *Emear*, thus, by-passing the chance to bestow a normal middle name altogether.

In moments of exasperation, Gerard craved to remove it, legally, in the courts. Just as his father had once done.

Others might have argued what all the fuss was about. Middle names rarely play a significant role in life. If only that was true, Gerry sighed. Yes. if you had a nebulous name, maybe. The sort, that was unlikely to trigger curiosity or ridicule. However, if you didn't then you, like Gerard, were unlikely to avoid the worst moments of school life. For in the playground, everything changes. There is nowhere to hide.

Learning to be invisible

When Gerard looked back, he guessed that it hadn't emerged as a problem until he was around nine or ten. Up to that point, Gerard had avoided the worst excesses of name calling during his early primary education. Interest largely lay with a little sniggering among one or two of the more perceptive members of year four. The ones who understood a bit about word association.

This wasn't helped by one particularly enthusiastic teacher at his school. Everybody knew Mrs. Cox had a love of all things historical. That included her choice of clothes. Most days, she breezed into the school looking like an extra from a *Charles Dickens* novel. One day she marched into Gerard's classroom with great bluster, to announce the start of a new Humanities topic: the family tree. Gerard was more than happy to hear all about his teacher's own fascinating family tale of great Dutch grandparents, their migration to the UK and their marriages to local Herefordshire farming folk. What young Pratt was not ready for, however, was the project that followed. Each pupil tasked with creating a large pictorial chart of their own family tree. Complete with large bold letters of their names; including middle names. He recalled Mrs. Cox looking puzzled at the appearance of the name *Eymer* on his chart.

"Look, everybody, Gerard has an unusual middle name in his family tree. How fascinating!"

Gerard's face crumpled in irritation. No, Miss, it really wasn't! All he wanted was for a hole in the floor to swallow him up. How he craved to have an ordinary surname. If only Miss would move on quickly to the next table. In that moment there was nowhere to hide from his own, glorious full name. But clearly, nobody else's name had intrigued her in the same way.

He'd tried to lessen the impact of this on his chart by changing the colour of the letters to an insipid green. Maybe the letters would fade quickly, and a squinting reader would quickly move on to another pupil's work. But no: Mrs. Cox was nothing if not thorough! She insisted on him going over these letters with a thick, black felt tip pen.

"You can't write your name in pale green, young man. How will anybody will be able to read it?" she exclaimed.

Exactly, Gerard cringed. How could she be so insensitive! By the time she realised he was crawling, ever deeper into acute embarrassment, the damage was done. The person known as *Gerard* had vanished and *Eymer Pratt* was born. A nightmare reincarnation of his former self. A suffocating shadow with the specific task of destroying his self -esteem and provide entertainment for some of the more easily amused children in his class.

There were other incidents before he left the school. He'd shared another memory with his wife from his time in year six. A young, flustered supply teacher had arrived that morning in a black tracksuit, to teach PE. Casting his eyes down the list of names before him, he stopped and started to snigger, uncontrollably. For reasons best known to him, he started to read out their full names. With great aplomb and what seemed an increased level of volume, he read out the words *Gerard Eymar Pratt*. He'd made the connection. Nothing was said, but his curious glance across at young *Pratt* confirmed his suspicions. Twenty-six faces in the room turned to follow his gaze. They looked at Gerard. The walls closed in on him as time seemed to grind to a halt.

Strange, he thought, all these years later, how such reminiscences, routed in the mind, refuse to disappear. Ever. He certainly hadn't forgotten.

"It's all in the past now," his wife would remind him. She understood the futility of saying any more. But it wasn't just located in the past. Twenty-three years on it was still eating away inside him. When they first met, she had failed to recognise it was a problem. Amy would rib him about it regularly. Even worse, she had brought the sort of surname to

8

their marriage that he would have loved to be born with. Smith. "Plain, extremely common and safe," he'd told her.

***

Secondary school life was always likely to be worse and so it proved. The access of full name lists to inquisitive classmates, in an era when children dutifully fetched registers and other documents for their teachers, (with a chance to secretly scrutinise details) would inevitably match *Eymer* with *Pratt*.

The result was several years of unrelenting 'piss-taking'. Some pupils almost forgot that he was once known as Gerard. "I'm a prat!" became a daily mantra that greeted him from several pupils who couldn't believe their luck. He wondered why his class teacher was wasting all that time in the *Personal and Social Education programme* on the importance of empathy. It wasn't working! Couldn't they see the connection?

Their response was to surreptitiously attach stickers to his back announcing his name to all and sundry. They chanted it in the playground. They goaded him with it when he travelled to and from school. They renamed the door of his locker, wrote over his class picture on the form room and inscribed his full named across the back of his sport's shirt. This group of boys considered *Pratt* much more fun than teasing the equally unfortunately named Annette Curtain in year eight! It got so bad that his mum had to come up to school to complain to his form tutor, Mr. Elliot.

He said he was sympathetic, but his eyes betrayed an indifference. "Some of the boys can get a little boisterous," he suggested. Mrs Pratt narrowed her eyes and said "Boisterous? Where I come from, we'd call it bloody bullying!"

Meanwhile, Gerard just slid further back on his chair and once again wished the ground would swallow him up.

***

As the time drew near to complete his endurance test at Redstone High School, he began to look forward to finally emerging from this life of ridicule. Gerry's plan was for his middle name to be carefully moth-balled, hidden away, hopefully, never to be used again. A closely guarded secret, even when he started work at the *Housing Department* in Stoke on Trent.

His toxic middle name vanished from all the official paperwork he filled in. It might have stayed that way, but for an unexpected romance and an emerging hobby. The hobby is not characterised by sensitivity or appreciation. Quite the reverse! It carried a multitude of dangers and it is certainly not for everybody. Football refereeing. It usually evokes a reaction from people who watch them in action. Brave, foolhardy maybe, but normally, unsympathetic. For some, openly hostile.

Such bewildering reactions lead to the inevitable question: Why do it? Even his small band of friends, many of whom shared his love of football, questioned his sanity. His hobby would be spending his spare time as a local league referee. What the hell was wrong with him? And that was just the responses that emerged from those who cared about him.

The answer lay somewhere between his obsession with the sport and the impact of a young woman who suddenly appeared, gloriously, in his life, one breezy October weekend. Jessica.

***

Whether it was driven by the tedious mediocrity of much of the play, or the mental instability of some of the players and managers, the morbid fixation some of them had with the match official seemed hypnotic to him.

Probing the limitations and weaknesses of referees was almost a science to some, as they over-analysed trends and statistics from the matches. Didn't they realise that referees were constantly judged, and their performances evaluated and marked by their peers at the FA? But referees names and statistics can be looked up and they were. Especially, when you were a soccer official.

It didn't take long for the word to get around. The young referee trying to disguise himself with a wispy brown beard, was none other than *Gerard Eymer Pratt*.

A love of football can place one in many challenging situations but taking such a name on to local league football pitches on Saturday afternoons was tantamount to character suicide! And it didn't get much better as he advanced through the professional leagues.

"Here comes Pratt, the twat in black" and other versions of it, were sung as terrace anthems. Gerard would spend many years craving respectability. At the pinnacle of his career, he was still having to deal with this.

For the love of the game

For as long as Gerard could remember, he'd loved football.

Like many boys and girls, his fascination sprung from his father's enthusiasm for the so called 'beautiful game'. The weekly ritual, of *Match of the Day,* played out by the gods of premier league soccer, was a Saturday night fixture at his house. He and his dad indulged in their own personal fantasies of fame and adoration as the players paraded their skills for the nation to drool upon and admire. Gerard's soccer fantasies surrounded his home club *Stoke City.* Given his team's performances, these fantasies were pretty modest. Dad was still dreaming about his old allegiance: *Galatasaray,* in Turkey. Living in the UK, it was a long time since he had cheered them on from the terraces. And, of course, neither were teams in the premier league. But they had come to terms with this reality. Instead, armed with an irrational sense of optimism, dad and son trundled off to the newly built Britannia Stadium to support *City.* In truth, this sense of hope was not based upon any tangible evidence. Simply the commonly held maxim that things couldn't get any worse!

The previous season, under the leadership of the esteemed former world cup winner, Alan Ball, had seen Stoke relegated to the third tier of English football. This, after finishing bottom of the old second division.

Surely the club, one of the original founding members of the football league, could bounce back amidst the mediocrity of their new fixture list? Alas not! A final position of fourteenth prove that the decline was still in progress. But it did cement something many fans understand about supporting a losing team. There can be a morbid obsession with attending such occasions. A fascination, almost akin to participation in a religious service. Their humiliation providing the backdrop for your act of sacrifice.

However, it was no surprise that dad eventually abandoned this ritual of weekly humiliation with the lure of TV soccer. It was still one of the few times when dad and Gerard would sit together during the week and enjoy a common interest. As *Sky TV* began to spin its seductive creed with a diet of programmes that became daily, there were far more of these moments of male bonding.

Dad was fond of telling everybody who would listen that he had played for his local pub team when he was younger. Albeit, briefly. "I was a tricky winger, like *Ryan Giggs*" he told Gerard.

Hard to believe, when you inspected his current physical appearance.

"I didn't look like I do now", he joked, defensively. "That was before I met your mother."

It was presented as though she should bear most of the blame for his early freefall into mid-thirties obesity. Was it really mum's fault for feeding him so well? These days he struggled for breath making the upstairs toilet run, let alone weaving his way through a sea of crunching tackles on a football pitch.

Gerard thought he looked older than the other dads he knew. Prematurely grey and glued to the sofa, like an old tabby cat that avoids wanting to go out. More fifty, than early forties, Gerard thought. He knew it wasn't his mum who had reduced him to a middle-aged lump. When he stretched back on the sofa, a perfectly formed circular ball appeared in front of his stomach.

It reminded Gerard of those hat-trick goal scorers who pushed the match ball under their shirts to claim it as a memento. But this ball wasn't sewn from leather. And there was nothing to celebrate here. It was built from the habits of nightly beer consumption, a high fat diet and virtually no meaningful exercise anymore.

***

As a teenager, Gerard was often found at the local park, re-enacting the latest drama from the premier league. On this stage he could be any player he wished to be. Well, in his dreams, maybe! When it came to analysing his ability, Gerard was realistic.

Mr. Beckett, one of the more sensitive of his PE teachers at school, had summed it up well. "You're not really suited to football, are you Gerard?" (inclusive teacher statement)

"You're fucking useless, Pratt!" *(Billy Cooper. Year 10 first team captain. NB Emotionally challenged teenager with emerging psychopathic tendencies)*

Learning to deal with such humiliation became a way of life for Gerard. Always one of the last boys to be picked for football teams at school. He could still taste the humiliation. The frustrated looks of other boys who didn't want him on their side. Yes, he knew his skill set was spectacularly ordinary. But so were the talents of so many other boys. The challenge for Gerard was how to match his unlimited energy for the game to his paucity of skill. In fact, virtually non-existent skills.

His friends, on the other hand, at least had had some ability. There was Kevin (talented, but lazy) Jim (physical, dogged, good passer of the ball) Sean (a bit of a goal poacher) and Phil (tall, good header of the ball but the turning speed of a bin lorry.) They would be joined by a late addition to the group, Raj, whose bone crunching tackling would bring another dimension, entirely. Gerard would have been delighted to settle for any one of these profiles. When they were young teenagers playing in the fields opposite, his mum would see them emerging often plastered in mud, on their way home for tea. Gerard's house was the first they passed. There would be Mrs. Pratt's initial ritual of berating Gerard for his dishevelled state when they all arrived at her door.

"Any chance of a drink, Mrs. Pratt. We're really thirsty?" the others would shout. They knew the answer was always a resounding yes, once their muddy boots had been slung into the porch. She loved to see her son enjoying the company of friends. But she worried about him. She observed how his lack of confidence coloured every judgement he made. Mum realised that the others largely tolerated her son instead of liking him. How she wished the boy carried around a little of his father's blind confidence.

Back in the kitchen, the drinks appeared with the anticipated extras. Her biscuit tin was an Aladdin's cave of sugary treats; always bursting with chocolate bars and biscuits. The appearance of this large red tin was guaranteed to bring expectant smiles to the faces of her hungry visitors.

In such moments, her mind was directed back to those formative years of marriage when discussions with her husband were often about children. She'd wanted more than one. Her partner was less keen. He kept reminding her what a difficult baby Gerard had been. All those sleepless nights and projectile vomit. Then, there was the cost.

In the end, she had given in to his resistance, but she continued to harbour thoughts about a larger family, well into her thirties. She looked around at the group of boys around her table and wondered about what might have been.

Grown-ups at play

The five lads may have gone their separate ways after leaving school, but they remained close friends. Kevin was still officially in full-time study; resitting one of his A levels, with hopes of starting a degree course in Business Studies at the local university. He had already begun homing his trading skills with a clandestine line in selling dodgy steroid tablets and some weed at local pubs. The others knew he was bright. He never touched the stuff himself. But, as yet, they hadn't anticipated the lengths he was willing to go to, to make money.

Kevin had sailed through his examinations at the end of year 11, with grade As and Bs in all subjects. It wasn't down to hard work: more a powerhouse memory for what was required by the exam boards. This had continued into his A-level courses.

However, GCSE results day had been a largely underwhelming experience for most of the other guys. Raj, Jim, Sean and Phil had failed to achieve any higher grades and had all left school.

They predictably drifted into low paid work; fledgling jobs characterized by unsociable working hours and limited prospects for career advancement. Still, at least there was now money coming into their pockets. For the time being, the future could take care of itself. Raj was clocking up ridiculous hours driving a van for a parcel delivery service. Jim was learning to lay bricks for a small building firm. While Sean was trying to establish himself as a car salesman in town. To everyone's surprise, Phil had found himself earning money from modelling clothing for an independent fashion company.

"That's not a real job", declared Raj, with blunt insensitivity. "More like selling yourself on the streets!"

"If you weren't such an ugly fucker, Raj, they might have asked you instead!"

The others had laughed and launched a collective restraint across Raj's broad shoulders. Phil wouldn't be doing much modelling with a broken nose. The gesture, more than words, sent a clear message. He'd become one of them. Phil, in particular, felt the need to extend a protective arm around the more fragile members of their little group. He recognised that Raj fell into a category of two. Gerard didn't need reminding who the other person was.

As for Pratt, things at school had turned out a little more hopeful. His collection of Grade Cs and a helpful connection through his mum with people at the local council, had carved out an opportunity in the Housing Sector. Not exactly an apprenticeship, but nevertheless, somewhere he could try to develop his modest potential.

Like many young men, he wasn't quite sure what he wanted to do with his life. Not yet. That would come soon enough. He proudly told the others he was now a *housing officer* but struggled to articulate what exactly he did each day. It seemed to entail an awful lot of tedious paperwork trails about individuals and families who struggled to put a roof over their heads. Still, he recognised the modest contribution he was making to the lives of people who were struggling. At least it was a job and as such, secured some respect, if not exactly the admiration, of his friends.

More importantly, it was a much-needed step towards establishing a more positive self-image.

One activity they all enjoyed was drinking alcohol. It seemed to form a back- drop to most aspects of their social life. Even Raj, a once devout Muslim, had embraced the pub culture and the central role that beer and other drinks played. The lads were able to combine these two interests in their lives, drinking and football, by supporting their despairing, yet loved, *Stoke City*. They thought here was something in the air at the ground that drove followers of the team to keep returning, in their numbers, for more. Was it loyalty, endurance or the constant need to be humbled that fostered this spirit? Or was it the bizarre logic that craved success on the field despite the evidence of everybody's eyes?

Whatever magic potion had been concocted, the guys continue to believe. After all, as Gerard frequently pointed out there had been successful times. This was usually greeted by blank stares. 1972 had been a good year (admittedly before they were all born). There were ten years in the premier league, during which the occasional Mancunian or Scouser scalp was taken and wins against the London elite. National attention had also been drawn to the deafening decibel levels, reported as the noisiest in the top division. But as other clubs with illustrious pasts will testify, clutching at such straws helps to ease the embarrassment of losing to non-league and lower division teams in the FA cup. And their notoriously loud chanting and singing didn't earn points as eventually the side they loved dropped back into the Football League.

Still, Gerard and friends loved the cult of matchday theatre. A circular ritual of pub/banter and expectation/disappointment and depression during the game/more alcohol and despair at the pub!

An observer scrutinizing the psychology of what was going on here might point to the special bond between fans and clubs; a relationship with deep-rooted needs at both ends.

There was always the eccentric and sheer lunacy which accompanied these days of drama. Phil's lucky pants, Jim's ten-year old club shirt and Gerard's precise timing about leaving his house and arriving at the ground. All this superstition in the face of overwhelming evidence to the contrary that it was all buffoonery. It couldn't nor did it alter what happened during the game. A keeper who can't catch the ball, centre -halves who can't win headers, midfielders who can't play an incisive pass to their own players and strikers who can't shoot. That's what stops your team from winning!

Apart from that, there's hope. Always hope and, of course, great humour! Terrace banter and chants often released the pent-up frustrations of people like Gerard, especially when it was self-deprecating. Raj, however, just preferred to hit people!

A sense of realism sank in when the boys arrived back at the pub to watch other people's teams, more successful teams, on TV. They chuntered as they watched but none of them had the heart to say the unsayable: Why can't our team play like that!

There was a moment in 2016 when the boys, like all fans of the under-dog, united as one to acclaim that rarest of football phenomena: a genuine miracle. How else to explain how the multi-millionaire signings from the top clubs were pushed aside by a team of journeymen from the East Midlands. Claudio Ranieri and his Leicester City. If you were a fan of that team there must surely have been some reflection that was there was indeed a God and heaven was draped in royal blue and white!

Raj

Raj gazed into the mirror and frowned. Screwing his face up was an automatic habit. A response to reality. He needed no reminders about the way he looked. A grizzled reflection. An unpleasant sight. Short, muscular, with a pitted, volcanic face that suggested it was about to explode into a thousand pieces at any moment. That was him in a nutshell and he knew it.

Others had noticed too; made the same observation about the crimson, lava shaped marks that lined his face like exploding magna. When he was young, the doctor had told him it was some sort of unusual skin complaint. With a temperament to match, it didn't draw people easily to him. They couldn't all be wrong. He struggled to disguise the fact especially when he became upset. And that was often. His face would crease up and his eyes would bulge.

Raj carried his considerable exasperation about life around like an angry mask. Many of these expressions were carved from a background of years of frustration. A young man burdened with multiple layers of tension. It had all started at home. A second-generation Muslim boy, with a white, English mother. She'd converted to Islam, after falling for an African buyer at work. The man from Kenya just swept her off her feet, she'd shared. Like his father, Najib, Raj was torn between conflicting cultures. His dad's response had been to learn the art of biting his lip, when confronted with some of the unsavoury challenges of life in the UK. Especially for an immigrant from Kenya.

This was particularly so with the racism he encountered at the company where he worked. He had tried to nurture his son with a similar sense of realism. But Raj had decided to adopt a different strategy for coping. Instead of trying to defuse the conflict situations he encountered and walking away from those who sought to antagonise him, he met it head on. Admirable, even courageous, some might argue, but a painful choice. Najib and his mother had lost count of the times their son had arrived home with a bloody nose and bruises.

Raj didn't feel comfortable hanging around with many of the boys he knew and as adulthood beckoned, he increasingly preferred to keep his own company. Driving a van for a living suited him just fine.

He wasn't close to his mother. He couldn't really understand why she had fallen for his dad. She seemed clever and talented. In Raj's eyes, he was neither. He wondered if she had settled for less than she might have done, in life? Raj grew to resent her lack of ambition and her slavish obedience to his dad's will.

Raj also felt alienated by his father's strict adherence to Islamic practices. When he listened to him trying to explain why the world was a difficult place for a Muslim to make their way, he recognised the sense of despondency in his voice.

"It wasn't easy for us, boy, back in Kenya. Those who live by the laws of Islam are just a small minority of the population, there, too. We always felt in danger."

There was a sadness behind Najib eyes. Was there also a lack of conviction about the advice he was now giving him? "Trust in the will of Allah, son," was his mantra for everything. But Raj had already stepped into this world outside his front door and realised that many of these dangers lay no further than the end of his street. Suspicion. Anger. Hostility. Prejudice. Was this really the hand of Allah at work? These experiences filtered his days with caution and foreboding. He had read the Koran; studied the life of the Prophet. But his conclusion was that Mohammed (Peace Be Upon Him) had lived in a very different land and time. And when things had got harrowing, even the Prophet had used violence.

Those challenges of the dust and desert in the Middle East, all those centuries ago, had failed to help Raj understand the cold indifferences of life in the industrial villages of contemporary Stoke-on Trent. This was seen most clearly in his reluctance to trust others.

He had struggled to make friends when he as young. Racist slurs and spiteful comments about his mother from both white and Asian boys had left him cautious about accepting people. Lashing out had become his preferred strategy for survival. But stoking his aggression was not going to help his transition into adulthood.

Although there was little interest in the subject at home, Raj thought he had found the perfect vehicle through which to direct his rage. Sport. However, brief flirtations with a boxing club and a fitness centre had failed to channel his anger through those mediums of exercise. He'd quickly fallen out with several users of the gym, having convinced himself that they were constantly staring at him. Provocatively. He left. The boxing club experience was even worse. It didn't go down well within his first month of membership when he broke the nose of the son of the coach because of some silly comment the lad had made about the size of Raj's own considerable nasal features.

It was almost by accident, that he'd drifted into hanging around with the placid Kevin and the other lads, down at the park. They were always down there playing football or generally hanging out. They often had other lads drifting into their kick-a-bouts.

Initially, he was hardly noticed. None of them gave him a hard time. After a while he was just another familiar face kicking a ball around with them. Gerard's friends didn't seem to mind him joining in. Nor did Gerard. It was good to have another outsider in their midst. It took the pressure off him, a little. But it also unearthed a skill that Raj didn't previously realise he had. One that the other lads came to respect. And respect was something his fragility desperately craved for.

From the first moment he launched himself, two-footed, like a guided missile, into an opponent's ankle, the others realised that Raj's tackling had something to offer to the game they loved. As long as it wasn't directed towards them!

"Save those two-footed ones for the teams we want to beat," Phil bellowed.

He was already thinking about them joining a competitive league in the area. Alongside Kevin's silky passing skills, Jim's interceptions and reading of the play, Sean's ability to score goals from any angle and Phil's gazelle-like leaps to head the ball, here was the final piece of this jigsaw. The mortar to cement a team who could take on the world. Well, at least, to take on another set of lads like them.

Somebody who could throw himself into a tackle like his life depended upon it, was surely worthy of a place in any side.

Outsiders

Then there was Gerard.

He'd grown up with these boys; been out there playing soccer with them since the beginning.

Unfortunately, his sporting CV read, simply: Nice lad. Reliable. Always keen. But, when it came to ability, and more specifically football skills, close to useless!

In the early days, his continuous presence was tolerated mainly because of the post-game provision of his mum's biscuits. However, that was stretching it when it came to team selection. The problem with Gerard was that he was so inept at the game, that just avoiding the mishap of constantly falling over on the pitch was an achievement. As he was a pal, they had tried to make allowances. Cover up his inadequacies by playing him in safe positions. Hide him in the middle of a crowded mid-field or position him as an extra full-back. But this was only possible when there were lots of additional lads joining them for a game. In truth, none of them really knew what to do with Gerard.

It all came to a head one sunny August evening when, sat outside their local pub, Kevin produced an advert he had pulled out of the local newspaper.

NEW SIX-A-SIDE LEAGUE REQUIRES TEAMS FOR SEPTEMBER

"This is exactly what we've been waiting for," he proclaimed. "What do you think, you lot. Shall we go for it?"

Kevin had laid down the challenge. This was their moment of sporting destiny. The fixtures were scheduled for Monday nights, so even workaholic Raj could make the games, as he finished early on the first working day of the week.

"The only thing we desperately need is a goalkeeper," observed Sean. All eyes turned to Gerard.

"What me? You must be joking," he replied in sheer panic.

They quickly realised the folly of this idea and began surfing their memory banks for an alternative candidate.

"Come on you lot. Only sensible suggestions," Kevin scorned.

"What about that tall lad with the shaved head who went in goal last week, down at the park?"

Phil's proposal was greeted with general approval.

"Does anyone know where he lives?"

Jim thought he'd seen him helping out around the building site. "I think he's labouring for one of the sub-contractors, down there. I'll catch up with him early next week and see what he thinks."

The lads left the house in a positive mood. Gerard was perturbed. Amid their enthusiasm, only one of them was struggling to see where they would fit in to this new team.

***

When the day arrived to play their first match, there was unbridled optimism within the gang. All that telepathic use of the ball to find team-mates, honed carefully, during years of practice at the park, would surely pay dividends.

A week before and without consultation, Phil had decided to appoint himself both manager and team captain, with an assurance that melted away other interested candidates. His trump card had been to secure a second-hand purple and silver kit, from his dad. It was certainly eye-catching, if a little garish.

"This will save us some money," he quipped but admitted that his dad's pub team were full of guys of a certain girth. However, it was a cheap option.

Sean pulled an enormous, rancid shirt from the bag. "Crikey. How big were these buggers!"

Meanwhile Jim was franticly searching through the shorts, looking for a pair without old skid marks that hadn't quite faded in the wash.

"I've even got a name for us too." Phil continued.

So it was that seven days later, they marched onto the AstroTurf under the banner of *The Dream Team*. A rather optimistic choice of name, but when pressed, none of the others had offered an alternative.

The opposition had arrived early. They were limbering up with serious intent. As they looked across at their colourfully kitted opponents, their contempt was clear to see. These lads from *Hasting Foundry*, had been playing in works leagues for years. They couldn't recall ever playing a team in purple and silver. This so-called *Dream Team* looked to them more like a fancy-dressed collection of tin men wrapped in over-sized purple gowns. A bunch of 'pre-Madonna' footballing nobodies.

At least *Hastings Foundry* represented something for them to be proud of. A place of work where all members of the team grafted for their living and could identify with what it stood for. There was nobody collecting subs here. The company had paid for everything. Their new bright red kit lit up the evening sky and amplified their purpose passion. But the *Dream Team?'* They had to be joking. Who the hell were this shower? They stood facing the *Hastings* boys, shirt sleeves draped around them like sagging tentacles, looking for all the world like young children dressed up in adult costumes. Their opponents had now completed their pre-match warm up and turned, stone-faced, to confront their challengers. They clearly meant business.

The five lads in purple lined up in front of their balding goalkeeper, Keith.

"My mates call me *slap,* he said to them, po-faced. ''I'll shout '*slaps*' when I'm coming out to collect the ball. OK, lads?"

The others seemed assured by these primitive, yet confident words and grunted their support.

Meanwhile, Gerard waited on the touch line. There was only one thing worse than being picked last and that was not being picked at all. However, there was one substitute allowed in these games and Gerard's disappointment was soothed, a little, by the possibility that he would fulfil this role and come on when the need arose. In the interests of winning the game, his team-mates hoped this wouldn't be too soon.

The referee arrived late, panting and vaguely smelling of whisky. He hardly inspired confidence.

"Can I ask the subs to run the line and give throw-ins?" he shouted across to the substitutes. "Any help with decisions would be well received," he added, hopefully.

Gerard proudly picked up the small red flag and stood on the touchline. "You can rely on me ref," he called out to the portly man in black. It felt like a monumental moment for Gerard. A window of opportunity.

Mr. Askew stood in the centre circle and blew his whistle to start the game. At least that is what the players thought was happening. He blew it again twice and pointed to something on the ground. Closer inspection revealed a large dog turd in the centre of the pitch.

"Shit!" shouted Sean.

"That's right, son" the referee confirmed.

"Shit" repeated Sean again.

As if it was a pre-rehearsed signal, someone in the sparse crowd was already moving towards them, armed with a poo bag. She looked a little guilty and quickly moved back to the edge of the pitch with the offending turds trapped in plastic. Her friend stood close by, keeping a tight rein on her canine accomplice. Meanwhile Sean was staring at a used condom lying close by.

"Bloody Hell. Doesn't anybody sweep these pitches?" the *Foundry* captain bellowed towards the official.

Mr. Askew shrugged his shoulders and found a tissue in his pocket. This second offending item was swiftly removed.

With the game finally started, the *Dream Team* were forced back by waves of red attacks. Within two minutes they were a goal down as the striker in red clipped the ball impressively over a stranded *Slap's* shiny head. Ten minutes later, it got worse. A collision between the keeper and Phil left another of the *Hastings* players the simple task of rolling the ball into an empty net. Meanwhile, their goalie, stood, shivering in the opposite goal. He'd had nothing to do for fifteen minutes. His designer gloves had hardly touched the ball. The big surprise was that *Hastings Foundry* had only scored twice. *Slap* was doing his best to keep the score down.

With the half-time whistle blown, the boys gathered in a huddle. Something drastic had to change if the *Dream team* were to avoid a drubbing. Step forward Raj.

Phil's team talk had failed to inspire much confidence. "They're running rings around us lads. We need to get hold of the ball and stop them playing."

Several confused faces stared blankly at their captain. Raj's face though, started to twitch, like some metaphoric change was about to erupt. He delivered a bold alternative. "Their striker won't be laughing when I deck him', he declared.

"Don't you get sent off, bruv," Sean pleaded. "It's difficult enough stopping these buggers with six players, without you disappearing for an early bath."

Meanwhile, Gerard stood quietly behind the guys, keeping his own council. As much as he'd enjoyed running the line for the referee, his heart was pumping for the chance to get on the pitch. As if reading his thoughts, Phil called him over for a chat.

"You're doing a brilliant job with the flag, Gerard. I'll try to get you on near the end."

Somehow Pratt didn't look convinced.

As the second half began, the opposition striker continued to tease them with his flicks and shimmies. That was until he attempted to nutmeg Raj. Big mistake. With the impact of an inter-city express train, Raj took aim and collided head-on with the red-shirted Number Nine.

Amidst the tangled arms and legs, only one of the players got up. The other lay prostrate on the ground, grimacing. Raj opened his arms in a display of pronounced innocence. The referee hadn't seen the incident. It had taken him an eternity to even arrive at the spot.

Wheezing and flustered, he blew for a drop ball. "Accidental collision!" he shouted with false certainty.

The team in red stared incredulously at him.

"You must be joking, ref!", one of them exclaimed. "That lad's a fucking psycho!"

"Watch your language, player," the official demanded.

Raj understandably took exception to this slight on his character. While the ref stooped to enquire about the physical state of the groggy *Hastings* striker, now sat up massaging his knee, Raj kneed the protesting player in the groin. His opponent recoiled in pain.

The referee turned around just in time to see the victim spring back. His retaliation was swift, lashing out with his fist towards his assailant. The red card was produced and quickly followed by a yellow one to the *Hastings* captain for more foul language.

The damaged player in red was gingerly helped from the pitch while Raj walked back to his central position. Despite his innocent expression, he was concealing the satisfaction of a job well-done.

"That should even things up a little," he said to Phil.

Short of both their best forward and their dismissed captain, the *Dream Team* seized their opportunity. As the whistle blew for the second half, they tore into their opponents with new-found vigour. Within three minutes, Phil had guided a header firmly into the net to reduce the deficit. Suddenly, the extra man was more than just a numerical advantage. It had put some belief into those who had been completely outplayed in the first half. Raj and Jim were now winning all of the midfield challenges. The remaining three outfield *Hastings* players were doing their best to keep a healthy distance from the Kamikaze tackler in purple. Sean was now enjoying the extra space up front and the opposition's replacement forward seemed to lack the appetite for a battle. All of a sudden, Sean was clean through again and slotted the ball past a startled goalkeeper to level the score.

Several other near misses were spurned. It seemed only a matter of time before a third goal came from the *Dream Team*. Then, out of the blue, Jim mysteriously collapsed to the ground holding his ankle.

"I think I've twisted it!" he boomed across to Phil.

Gerard's heart-beat quickened. Could his moment have arrived? With a glance that betrayed his worst fears, Phil beckoned the substitute across.

"Gerry. You're on", he whispered in his ear. "We're going to win this. Just, don't do anything stupid."

Gerard scampered on to the pitch to shake the departing Jim's hand. He looked across at their opponents. They looked much bigger, more menacing, up close. Nevertheless, His brittle confidence grew wings and, with shirt sleeves flapping in the breeze, he replaced his team-mate. Five minutes to go. What an opportunity!

Unfortunately, his head was still clouded in thoughts of glory as the *Foundry* player broke away from his own penalty box. He sped through the space previously occupied by Jim.

By the time Gerard had realised the imminent danger, he was directly in front of him. Gerard looked into the whites of his eyes, as they faced each other on the edge of the penalty area. With a deep breath Gerard Pratt stuck out a leg to take a swipe at the ball and missed completely. The only thing he connected with was the opponent's left calf. The player sank to the ground as if he'd been shot and rolled around dramatically to emphasise the foul.

"Penalty, ref!" his team-mates screeched as one.

But was the tackle inside or outside the box? Unfortunately for Gerard, the referee was still getting his breath back from a previous attempt at sprinting across the field and had stayed in the other half, hovering well behind the incident. But a decision needed to be made. He placed the whistle to his lips and pointed to the penalty spot.

"Bloody hell, Pratt. What did you do that for? You Moron!" Jim shouted.

There were no words of support to ease the seriousness of what he had done. Gerard hung his head in shame. The others stared daggers at their substitute.

The penalty was thumped into the right corner of the net, as *Slap* dived the wrong way. 3-2. The goalkeeper quickly retrieved the ball. He kicked the goal post in disgust and shouted something unrepeatable at Gerard.

The final whistle was blown shortly afterwards. It signalled much rejoicing among those in red. Gerard slinked off to the touch line, head held in shame. His team-mates didn't need to amplify the issue.

Nevertheless, they all had their say, while getting changed. Later in the pub, Jim and Phil were still going on about lousy tackles that had cost them the game. And they weren't talking about the ones dished out by Raj.

An unexpected visitor

Gerard's family had known the Stones' for many years. A decade before, they had been next door neighbours in Hanley.

Gerry's dad and Mike Stone had got on well. They shared an interest in gardening, developing something of a friendly competition with each other, when it came to growing vegetables. They would sometimes meet up on Friday nights, at the *White Horse Inn* to chew the cud over a few beers. Gerry's mum, Leslie and Mike's partner, Amy, had also become friends. They'd become involved in *The Parent Teacher Association* at the local school and attended the same *Weightwatchers* class there, on Tuesdays. Occasionally, they would even catch a film together at the local cinema and Amy and her two girls regularly popped in for a cup of tea and cake after school. It wasn't only Gerard's football chums who appreciated his mum's baking.

All this changed when the Stone family moved away to a village, outside Stoke, six years later. Mike's ceramics factory was moving to a new site and the offer was attractive. They didn't see as much of each other afterwards and drifted apart.

Then out of the blue, Leslie received a call from Amy. One thing led to another and Gerard's parents informed him that the Stones' would all be coming around on Sunday, for tea. He didn't react. He could vaguely remember the older daughter, Jessica, from school, but that was some time ago.

"Please. Try to be here, Gerard. They'd love to see you" his mum implored him. It wasn't as if he usually had much else to do on a Sunday afternoon.

When Jessica walked through the front door that October weekend, he went weak at the knees. Standing before him in the hallway was a beautiful, tall, athletic young woman. She greeted him with an assured "Remember me, Gerry?"

"Well, not like that", he was tempted to say but satisfied himself with a smile and a polite "Hello."

What had happened to that skinny, shy girl who was always hiding behind her mum? It was something of a shock, how much Jessica had changed. As they chatted, her confident demeanour and calm authority reduced him to jelly. When he finally composed himself, the conversation which followed vividly illustrated why their lives were heading in opposite directions.

"Someone told me you were still hanging around with those lads from school," she probed. "Thought you'd have moved on from all that, by now."

He mumbled something incomprehensible about football practices and regular meet ups at the local pub.

Then Jessica shared her first bombshell. Gerard was enthralled. She had been signed-up to play football for *Hanley Ladies*. They even had a regular report on the inside of the local free paper. He'd seen it!

"Yes. I love playing football," she continued. "In fact, I've also signed up because they want young women to train as referees."

Bombshell Number Two! A budding referee in the making.

This really took him by surprise. So much so, he realised he was fighting hard to avoid staring at her. He couldn't help noticing how Jessica had blossomed into a voluptuous young woman. In fact, such was the mesmeric state she had reduced him to that he sat there, nodding blindly at everything she said.

Before the Stone family had even dived into his mum's homemade chocolate cheese-cake, Gerard had screwed up his courage to ask if they might meet up, sometime. He spluttered, "I'm keen on getting into refereeing too" and mithered an excuse about wanting to look over some of her refereeing paperwork. He cautiously reached for his mobile phone. "Maybe, I can text you?"

To his shock, she agreed. "Just one thing, Gerry," she said. "I'd prefer it if you stopped ogling me! It's embarrassing."

Gerard blushed. "Sorry Jessica. You know how our minds are wired."

She broke into a faint smile. He needed to change the subject. He was already looking forward to their next encounter.

***

Gerard Eymer Pratt sat on his bed, fiddling with his phone. His mind was racing. He re-read the message he'd sent to Jessica earlier that day. Had he gauged the situation correctly? He guessed that inviting himself to her house to look over refereeing training documents did sound a little dull. But wasn't the idea safe territory for her? He could mention some of the articles he had read about the management of football. Kill two birds with one stone, so to speak. Maybe it was to his advantage that he knew more than she might think about the subject. Despite his normal reticence for risky manoeuvres, he had decided it was worth a go. She might even be impressed.

Jessica's eventual response took him by surprise. She offered an alternative. Why didn't they meet up for a curry in town?

Was this a date? Did she already like him? Too many questions! There might not be another opportunity and he hadn't been on a date for some time. Almost eighteen months. Assuming that didn't include Charlotte, at work. Not his finest hour. They had met at the Housing Department after she'd started there as a temp. A cautious girl, with long black hair and somewhat guarded eyes. He thought he was making an impression. A quiet drink at the *Weaver's Arms*. Reaching for some money in his pocket. Instead of a £10 note, a packet of strawberry flavoured condoms emerged and fell to the floor. The look on her face. His cheeks had turned the colour of the contraceptives. Angry words humming in his ears as she disappeared from the bar. Gerard could understand how it might look. But he hadn't assumed anything. He'd had them for some time. Three years, in fact. They were getting close to the use-by date. Just in case, he'd thought. "You plonker, Pratt." He could hear the words echoing in his head.

He knew he wasn't comfortable around attractive women. Decision making had always been a tricky business when it came to dealing with the opposite sex. Gerard consoled himself with the knowledge, that he wasn't the only young man who struggled to read the subtleties of the female mind.

***

Pratt cast his phone aside and stretched out on the bed. The subdued light of early evening lit up one side of his bedroom as he looked across at the main wall. The cacophony of his modest life seemed to be captured in the pictorial memories, pinned to the magnolia paper. A framed picture of the Stoke City League cup-winning team of 1972 stared confidently back at him. Another, more recent photo, of *The Dream Team*, hung modestly alongside it. A team, he knew, he had hardly ever played for, but there was still some pride. A commemorative plate adorned with the face of Stoke City's most famous player, *Sir Stanley Matthews; stood* proudly on the shelf below alongside a selection of old football programmes. Further around the wall was a fading picture of Angelina Jolie from the film *Beowulf,* peering provocatively from her gold body paint. A poster of *Coldplay* completed the display.

"Maybe, I'm just caught in a time-trap" he mused. "What I need is a new image." Even some of his football buddies, down the pub, would have nodded their heads in approval.

He was still thinking about what this makeover might entail, when he picked up his mobile and replied to Jessica's invitation.

Spice and romance

Gerard was like his friends when it came to food. More a fish and chip man than a lover of foreign delicacies. Much to his father's disappointment, that even included some of his dad's favourite Turkish recipes. He just didn't warm to spicy food, whether it was Turkish, Chinese or Indian cuisine. All this, despite his mum's efforts to make their meals at home more varied. Gerard's only recollection of Indian food was the creamy coconut chicken *Korma* he had eaten at a party the previous year.

Jessica's suggestion was going to be a challenge.

Despite his offer to pick her up, she had decided to meet him at the restaurant. He made sure he was early and hovered outside the building. She arrived ten minutes late.

"Sorry Gerry. Traffic. I can call you Gerry, can't I?"

He smiled. In that moment Jessica could have addressed him by any name she chose. Even Eymer Pratt.

As he sat opposite her in the *Bombay Delight,* that Friday evening, he should have recognised the danger signs. He was a young man out of his comfort zone. Someone who knew virtually nothing about the restaurant's culinary delights. And he so wanted to impress her. His pockets hid a carefully created list of miscellaneous trivia about refereeing. Leave nothing to chance, he'd concluded.

Gerard had earlier pulled out his cream jacket from the wardrobe and new, starched jeans for the occasion and chosen the expensive shirt his parents had bought him for his birthday. The dark red flowered one. His mum had told him he looked rather suave in it. Copious amounts of hair-gel had helped to sweep his brown locks away from his face. Finally, over-indulgence with his recently acquired after-shave *Hidden Zones* had spread its scent to parts of his body it should have remained away from. Before leaving his house, he'd glanced at the full-length mirror in the hallway and concluded that he looked quite a catch!

It would surely have been too big a risk to try and change the venue. He just had to make the best of things and avoid embarrassing himself.

He watched Jessica as she scrutinised the menu with confidence. The waiter stood next to her with his notebook ready.

"I think I'll go for the *Dhall* soup as a starter and *Jhinga Bhuna* for the main course, please. Can you let me have some mushroom *Pilau* rice and a side dish of *Bhindi Bhargee, too?*"

Without pausing for breath, she turned to him. "How about you, Gerry?"

Gerard froze as he perused the list of unrecognisable dishes. His self-esteem demanded something exotic to impress her with. As he read through the menu for a second time, the waiter cleared his throat and tried to hide his impatience. Gerard eventually turned towards the man.

"What would you recommend?"

Immediately, he realised the potential for disaster. But it was too late.

"Do you like authentic hot dishes, sir?"

"Mm. Oh yes." Gerard delivered these words with a strained smile.

"Then try this one, sir. It's one of our specials."

The waiter pointed to the house specialities. *Chilli Tandoori Chicken.* Apart from the mention of chicken, he didn't really recognise any of the other ingredients read to him.

"Go for it, Pratt! No time for hesitation," he whispered to himself.

He really should have spotted the symbols lying underneath the description of the dishes sooner.

"And I'll have the same soup as the lady." he added. "Three chillies" he read, as the waiter disappeared with their order.

He realized it was too late. Gerard was convinced that such a confident choice would ingratiate him into Jessica's affections. He'd just have to get on with it.

Gerrard reckoned he'd be safe with soup and plunged his spoon into the bowl. Each mouthful started to burn with greater intensity. Clearing his throat, he launched into a coughing fit, and abandoned the table, knocking his bowl over and spilling the remaining *Dhall* down his trouser leg. A yellowish-green stain glowed, embarrassingly, from the area of his crotch.

Gerry sought refuge in the men's room. Once inside he devoured several handfuls of sink water. He hoped it was drinkable. The tap was left running as Gerard frantically attempted to wipe the stain away with the aid of his referee crib sheet. There were no paper towels. It only made it look worse. Using his hands to best disguise his humiliation he sheepishly returned to find that Jessica had finished her soup.

"You Ok Gerry?" she probed. "It wasn't that spicy, was it?"

He delayed answering the question and took a swig of ice-cold *Cobra*.

"Yeah. Just got something caught in my throat."

The approaching sounds of sizzling chicken rescued his dignity as the trolley arrived with their main courses. Jessica's prawn dish was perched under a crackling wok of scorching chicken. Gerry looked at it with curiosity and fear.

"Another pint of *Cobra* sir?"

The waiter brought the drink together with a small dish of yoghurt. "Try this," he said, with the authority of someone who was familiar with these customer symptoms. Jessica picked through the carefully chosen sundries she had ordered and passed the additional *Naan* bread and rice to her companion.

If Gerard thought that the soup was hot, he was in for an even greater shock. It only took two mouthfuls of the chilli-laced meat to send tears running down his cheeks. He reached for the napkin to wipe them away.

"You've gone a strange colour, Gerry. Your face is clashing with that shirt of yours."

He'd made such a *tit* of himself over the soup, he just had to finish the main course. The yoghurt was consumed with such aplomb that another two tubs were ordered. With the tears continuing to cascade down his increasingly ruddy face, he somehow managed to eat most of the dish. Gerard sat back, exhausted.

Jessica watched him, trying not to smirk. It was obvious he wasn't used to this food, so why on earth had he ordered such a hot dish?

She reached across to grab his hand. "Did you do this for me? Bless you, Gerard Pratt"

They both started to laugh. As she linked arms with him on the way to the car park, Gerard reflected that the evening was ending rather better than he could have expected.

And then she leaned across from her car and planted a kiss on his cheek. "We must do this again," she said. 'But maybe not in an Indian restaurant!'

***

Two months later, they were no longer just sharing food and exchanging views about the art of refereeing. They were an item. When the lads arranged to see a *Status Quo* tribute band at their local pub, Kevin and Phil said they'd bring their girl-friends. They could have fallen off their bar stools when Gerard announced that he would bring somebody along, too. That would be a first! He showed them a picture of Jessica. When he told them what she did, Kevin, Jim, Raj and Phil were speechless. Sean launched into a speech about the hand of destiny. Their nerdy friend with two left feet falling for a talented footballer. You couldn't make it up! They mocked him mercilessly. The only shock was that the player concerned was female.

"Must admit, I thought you were gay mate!" announced Kevin with brutal insensitivity.

Only Gerard knew that Jessica's love of football extended beyond just playing for her local ladies team. He didn't mention to the others that she had also felt driven to start taking refereeing qualifications through the local *Football Association*. Training to be a proper official. Wow!

Two years later, when it emerged that Jessica had progressed sufficiently to be entrusted with line duty in the higher echelons of non-league football, they were speechless.

"Bloody hell" said Sean, with his usual gift for stating the obvious. "She's going to be famous and she's going out with you, Pratt."

Gerard could only sit and absorb the collective admiration. He wasn't used to people saying pleasant things about him. He was now even convinced that there was a God after all and all those humiliations in the past had been worth it.

"Yes," he continued with a bewildered expression. "Conference and Midland league games. She's even is going to feature on TV, next month. First round of the Women's FA Cup. She'll be officiating at a woman's professional game, chosen by *Sky*." Just sharing this statement made him prouder and more besotted with her than ever.

"So, what does she see in you, Pratt? Does she think you're loaded?"

Kevin's withering comment failed to wound him. He knew what blokes were like. With good grace, he simply explained to them that he really didn't know and actually didn't care. This wasn't true. He'd been just as bemused about her interest in him for some time.

Rules of the game

The more Gerard read about refereeing, the more absorbed he became. He tried to familiarize himself with every aspect of the role. To aid him in this he sent away to the *Referee's Association* for more information. The mandatory examination of physical fitness for men (known as the *Cooper* test) intrigued him. All those minimal sprinting and running times to be met. He knew he could demonstrate most of these comfortably. But some of the referees he'd watched in the past would surely have struggled to pass these. He ploughed through the information about progression through the different levels of competence. Then there was the money. The renumeration figures caught his eye. From £20 a game in park football up to a salary of around £70,000 in the Premier League. Not bad, at all for something you loved to do! Picking up his pen, he placed a large tick in the self-assessment form next to fitness levels. He may have been inept with a ball on the field, but he was as quick as anyone in running across it.

'I could do this', he thought.

Gerard ploughed through the other sections of the report. He tried to self-access his answers honestly. Whatever he claimed he could do, would certainly be tested by the training experts. There was so much about the management of this sport that he didn't yet know. He carefully studied the seventeen laws of the game. So many decisions to be made where his judgement about what he'd seen would be crucial. Whether it was the nuances of the off-side rule, playing the advantage to reward a fouled attacker, or how to add time on to the normal ninety minute length of match, he marvelled at the precision and exactitude of it all. Gerard felt that he was beginning to understood the game in a way he could never have grasped through his limited playing skills. He began to make copious notes about game management and discussed it with Jessica whenever he had an opportunity.

She wasn't entirely convinced. "You don't have to pretend you're into all this, you know. I don't need impressing, Gerard."

He'd realised that she wasn't naive. But Jessica hadn't fathomed the extent of his interest. It was bordering on the obsessive. He started to see the game he loved as a complex jigsaw of angles, intentions, statistics and judgements. Despite Jessica's taunts, he sensed support in her voice. During quiet moments of intimacy, she hinted that Gerard was different from the other guys she knew. More sensitive; more thoughtful. He listened attentively to her exasperations and celebrated the successes she enjoyed. "Yes, he's a bit compulsive, even eccentric," she thought. "But no-one's perfect."

Gerard knew that much of this was true but nevertheless, rejoiced in his good fortune. She liked him. That was enough. When his parents found out they were overjoyed.

"Oh Gerard!" his mum exclaimed, with a big sloppy kiss on his cheek. "You're a dark horse, aren't you!"

They constantly asked after her. He knew that they too, were bemused. Even so, they couldn't hide their pleasure in seeing their son so happy.

Gerard started going to watch her playing for *Hanley Ladies*. She was an impressive sight to behold on the pitch. Few of her colleagues could match her sporting elegance. Strong, athletic and effective in both penalty boxes, she prowled around the pitch like a wild cat seeking out her prey. He particularly admired her ability to make the right choices when in possession of the ball and the timing of her runs off the ball. All the things he found incredibly difficult, himself.

Although she played in midfield, Jessica had an eye for goal. Her tally of goals was already in double figures for the season and it was only November. It was no coincidence that she had been encouraged; targeted by her club and team-mates to officiate at other matches as well as play. Jessica rarely seemed flustered by illegal challenges on her, or decisions that didn't go her way. He could see what everybody else did. That her ice-cool temperament would be ideally suited to refereeing.

Gerard was painfully aware that he would never replicate any of her skills on the pitch. He could only dream of performing like this. But the role of referee seemed to offer him another dimension. As long as he maintained his fitness levels, continued to study the laws of the game diligently and developed an appropriate temperament for officiating matches, there was hope he could progress to a high level.

After all, when he thought about all those poor refereeing performances that he'd watched at Stoke games or on TV, why shouldn't he do better? Many of these men had emerged from complete obscurity, just like him. He must have half a chance! He told himself that you didn't have to be an ex-player to move into officiating. Just a thick skin and the will to survive.

***

The forms he had been waiting for finally arrived from the *Referees Association.*

After tea, he retreated to his bedroom and laid them out on his bed. Two hours later, Gerard got up and confidently stretched his arms back above his head. He stared at the completed application form in front of him. It had taken much longer to fill in than he'd expected. There were lots of questions about his background and how much experience he had in football. Some of his answers were thin, to say the least. Occasional appearances for a six-a-side team that nobody had ever heard of and voluntarily running the line when no one else was available, didn't look over- impressive. His *achievements in football* column remained blank. Gerard didn't have any. All he had going for him was an irrational desire to make it as a referee. He consoled himself with the fact that few professional players or coaches moved into refereeing. The people who did had a different background story to tell.

"I bet most of them didn't have achievements," he mouthed, silently to himself. "Who really are these blokes who trot out to referee football matches?"

He researched as many profiles as he could find on *Wikipedia* and other on-line sources. A bewildering range of background professions and jobs emerged. Several of them were ex-army or police officers. It made sense. Keeping the warring factions apart. But how would he cope? He wasn't aggressive or macho. What did he have to offer? Was there was room in the organisation for a housing officer from Stoke-on-Trent?

***

Three weeks after posting his letter back to the *Referees Association* in Staffordshire, he received a reply. They thanked him for his enquiry but felt that he needed to invest more time volunteering in a range of amateur games. Schools, local charity matches, and the like were all given as examples. Once that was in place, they could re-consider his application.

Jessica knew what they meant. She gently tried to spell out the importance of building a portfolio of evidence to him before contacting them again.

Gerard set his mind on un-earthing every kind of football match in his locality and busied himself contacting all of the organisations to see if they would be prepared to let him help.

There were some positive responses. One of the primary schools was struggling to find someone to ref the boy's Year Six team. Unfortunately, he would have to fund the CRB check on his suitability to work with children himself. The cheek of it!

One of the works leagues was desperate to take on younger candidates. In fact, any candidates! You even got paid for this. It wasn't a fortune and you had to buy your own kit, but he saw this as a good investment. And it wasn't phrased quite so negatively. The word *opportunity* was emphasised a number of times to 'those of strong character.' Was he strong-minded? You bet he was! They disguised the fact that four Saturday

League referees had resigned that month, citing various combinations of racism, ridicule and threats of violence, as reasons why they were retiring from the role. Gerard glimpsed an opening.

Six months and thirty-two games later, Mr. Gerard Eymer Pratt had secured the interview he had been working for.

***

Standing outside the office building in Burton, he sniffed the morning air. The sweet smell of roses swept across from the flower boxes lining the steps. It heightened his sense of expectation. Armed with his folder of statistics, match dilemmas and anecdotes, the lad from the Potteries strode purposely into his interview. Sitting opposite Gerard was someone from the *Staffordshire Football Association* who examined him from head to foot, like he was preparing to purchase a prized animal.

"Mm," he uttered with open prejudice. "Quite short, aren't you?"

"Almost five foot seven," he responded, straightening his back.

Without blinking an eye, the interviewer added, "How old did you say you were, again?"

"Twenty-two".

"You look younger, son. I trust you're pretty thick-skinned. You'll need to be!"

Mr. Brough proceeded to fire a myriad of questions in his direction, nodding, affirmatively, as he listened to Gerard's replies. And Gerard Eymer Pratt was certainly well prepared. Despite the official raising an occasional eyebrow in a gesture of surprise, he closed the papers in front of him and removed his glasses.

"Let's give it a go, shall we. See how you get on. And a word of advice, lad. Don't be intimidated by some of the players and coaches. Many of them subscribe to that old Bill Shankly saying about football being more important than life and death itself. Remember: it is!" He smiled with his full set of gleaming dentures and went off to find an FA outfit and accessories booklet so Pratt could order some *real* kit.

Gerard felt euphoric. He stood up to stretch his legs and caught sight of himself in the large wall mirror behind him. He had to admit he wasn't exactly an imposing figure. It was at that precise moment that Gerard Eymer Pratt decided it was time to grow a beard. Well, at least he would try to do so. He wasn't confident that the patchy shadow around his chin would constitute much of a growth but maybe some facial hair would create an image of greater authority. And as such, help him to keep apart those belligerent factions, both on and off the pitch.

***

Later that night, he shared his refereeing ambitions with his friends.

"You two lovebirds having some sort of competition to see which of you can get to the top of the refereeing ladder first?" Sean joked.

The penny still hadn't dropped. How else was the cumbersome Pratt going to make his own little mark on the world of soccer? The full extent of his interest came pouring out like a religious confession. His correspondence with the FA; his willingness to referee, wherever he could find somebody who needed one; his desire to officiate at a higher level. For once, the boys listened without the need to inject infantile humour.

Finally, Phil stood up with collective words on behalf of the others.

"I say good luck to you Gerard. I'll drink to that!"

And with a rousing "Your round, Pratt," Gerard publicly consecrated his mission by buying them something to toast him with.

Moving on

The Monday evening games continued to take place and Gerard found himself spending much more time running the line rather than playing. The others had long forgiven him for his misdemeanour on the opening night of their first match and he was still encamped as the *Dream Team's* official substitute. They suspected that his mind was now elsewhere and that playing for the team was more an additional bonus. Occasionally, he'd get some minutes on the pitch, but only when one of the others was injured. He'd learned to play it safe: avoid stupid tackles in his own penalty area and as soon as he got the ball, to pass it immediately to one of his colleagues who knew what to do with it. But something strange had happened. He was starting to enjoy his role as a linesman, and on two occasions, emergency referee, far more than actually playing. The other lads had noticed. He'd lost that excruciating look of disappointment when he didn't get on the pitch till the last few minutes.

"You all right, Gerard?" they would query him. "Not sulking, are you?"

"I'm ok guys. Quite happy being on standby."

Gerard was busy expanding his curiosity about the kind of reactions he was receiving from opposition players and bystanders, when acting as a linesman or referee. He wanted to better understand the psychology of this phenomena. There was always somebody contesting even minor decisions, like throw-ins. He couldn't understand why.

"For God's sake, it's only a bloody throw in!" he wanted to screech.

He blamed much of this competitive madness on the professional game. Every action was now challenged; deemed to be crucial, provoking so many hysterical responses. It was TV that was fuelling it. Everybody just needed to calm down. Grasp some perspective, he'd concluded.

He watched how the referees in his league had to endure the ridicule and contempt of players when disciplinary cards were issued, or controversial goals were scored. All the time he was cutting his teeth for the time when he stepped out of these elementary games and into a limelight where the stakes would be much higher.

***

Two more summers passed. The *Dream Team* had improved since those early days. Having held their own during the previous couple of campaigns, they were now battling it out at the top of Division Four. Jim had packed in playing because of knee problems and Raj had just served his second suspension of the season for violent play. Gerard, meanwhile, had found himself increasingly unavailable to play his role of the virtually unused sub. There were now other matches to referee. Not that the lads struggled to replace him. Now they were doing well, there were plenty of others who were happy to take his place. He continued to meet up with some of the boys down at the local pub on most Fridays.

Although he was still seeing Jessica, it was less often than he wished. He did not realise it, but the relationship had certainly plateaued. One night, as they enjoyed a meal in town, his girlfriend seemed troubled. She went to great lengths to emphasise how much she valued Gerard as a friend. Other men might have scented something looming. For Gerard, it arrived like a sudden thunderstorm. The penny only dropped when she floated the idea of not seeing quite as much of each other in the near future.

"We're both so busy, with work, sport and refereeing, etc. these days. You know how it is."

Gerard didn't know. Was this about their sexual relationship? He knew it had been problematic, but he was doing his best! He wasn't as experienced in this area as she was. Had his fumbling performances between the sheets; his tentative foreplay; those premature ejaculations, brought her to this?

Gerard recalled how she always looked disappointed after they had had sex.

He refocused. Her hollow words of support fell upon empty ears. She knew he'd only had one serious girlfriend before, and that liaison had barely lasted three months. Eventually Jessica revealed the real shock.

"The thing is, Gerry...I've met somebody else. At the club. You know how it is." She was using that phrase again. Jessica tried to continue. "It's not really happening for us as a couple, is it?" Before he could summon a response, she blurted out "At least not for me."

And with those words, she faded away from his life. Gerard realised that there was little else to say. Like a product beyond its sell by date, he had been disposed of in favour of a shiny new model. Unceremoniously dumped was how Sean had interpreted it, when they met up in the pub.

"It's happened to me lots of time," he added.

This did not provide the comfort Gerard needed.

That evening, in the solitude of his own space, he tried to think what he should do next. He guessed that he wouldn't be able to change her mind. Anyway, when the disappointment had lifted, Gerard realized he would just have to get on with things. He had his new career to concentrate on and nothing was going to deflect him from his ultimate aim: to qualify as a league referee. He fell asleep dreaming about walking out onto the pitch wearing a league referee's badge, ready to facilitate the football he could only dream of playing. And Jessica was standing behind him in the dugout, cheering him on with pride!

***

Despite his positive words and a brave reaction to outside interest, breaking up with Jessica had been a huge blow. She was so much more than just his girlfriend. She had become his confidante, his advisor and best friend. Jessica had restored his fragile self-esteem and helped him to be more assertive with others. For that, Gerard would forever be grateful. He listened to everyone around him who had an opinion about what had happened. They were mainly sympathetic but told him it was inevitable. Eventually, Pratt resigned himself to the situation. He would adjust to his new, single status by focussing even more intensely on his passion for refereeing.

***

He moved quickly through the *Football Association* initial levels of refereeing, receiving good reports from his mentors and assessors. They all drew attention to his enthusiasm and unflustered manner.

Gerard's performance feedback eventually projected him into the world of semi-professional matches. The big difference he now faced had less to do with any new additional skills he would be required to employ. It was more about the increased size of the crowds. There were always the smaller clubs who struggled to attract many souls to watch them. Often rural teams or city clubs whose great moments all lay in the distant past. Like his own team, *Stoke City*. However, some of these sides attracted over a thousand people to their fixtures. Sometimes nearer three. This required more sophisticated radar skills from the *man in the middle.*

"Remember the eighteenth law of the game," his mentor, Matt Jones would say to him. "If you don't know what to give, use your common sense and give what you *think* you've seen."

They had been warned about how refereeing decisions could provoke mob reactions in a crowd. How the mood in the ground could change quite radically, on a single refereeing decision. There was also the new experience of hearing orchestrated responses from the spectators, rather than just individual rants. Groups of observers, united in their recognition of his astuteness and wisdom (he hoped) or, more often, bonded by their derision of his judgements.

A game too close to home

The years continued to pass. It was now five football seasons since Jessica had been a major part of his life. Gerard had risen to level three refereeing status; running the line and providing standby support for football league matches. He knew that the serious business of senior football now beckoned. How he craved to referee at his be-loved *Stoke City*, but this was not going to happen. He had declared his allegiance to the Potteries club on paper and he realised that the Football League monitored the possibility of favouritism very seriously.

***

But something not dissimilar did unfold. Although now buried at the back of his mind, it had always been a possibility. Some of those who knew him well joked that it was almost inevitable. Destiny conjuring up the sort of un-expected encounter that shakes the memory banks and releases all those deep-rooted emotions from the past. Vivid, heartfelt memories, that float back into one's head like the sudden arrival of waking birds. When he told Phil and Raj down at the pub, they laughed and said unpleasant things about giving her a hard time. After all she had dumped him almost five years ago.

"Let her know how you still feel, mate" said Phil.

"Ignore any feisty challenges on her. Let her feel the pain, bruv" added Raj.

The truth was that nothing could be further from his mind. Gerard still harboured a deep fondness for his ex, even if they had both moved on.

It had been a late change. The game should have been refereed by another official, but a combination of factors led to him responding to the urgent request from the local Football Association. The names of the teams barely registered at first. But then the venue of the game brought it all back. *Hanley*

Ladies Football Club. Of course, he realised! A time of great happiness for him. Jessica. Should he say something to the officials? Declare their past relationship? Turn down the plea from the *Referee's Association?*

"But she may not even be playing there anymore' he deliberated. 'She could be injured or may have moved on to another club."

On the morning of the match, he considered ringing her. He still had an old contact number. But that was against professional protocol. Inside, he knew he couldn't make contact. All that training he'd received about avoiding bias and favouritism, was crystal clear. He would have been required to declare an interest in one of the teams; and a specific player, still close to his heart. It would have ensured he was no longer authorised to proceed with the game. Then what would they do without a referee? But he knew the real reason. He wanted to see her again. Gerard wondered if she had changed, much? Eighteen months back, he was still looking out for Hanley's results but that had eventually stopped.

Almost certainly, she didn't know he would be refereeing the match. It would be a surprise for her too. Could there be an opportunity to speak to her after the game? So many questions.

***

With these thoughts still bombarding him, he turned up on the day with his heart pounding. Gerard changed into his match outfit and checked his sanction cards and equipment. He was ready for action. Breathing heavily, he completed his pre-match stretching routine before being interrupted by the customary knock on the door.

"OK, Ref. Teams are ready!"

The bearded man in black trotted out onto the pitch. He scanned the *Hanley* players for evidence of her. Sure enough, at the far end of the pitch, crashing in practice shots at her goalkeeper was the unmistakable image of the woman he once loved. She looked a little older, with shorter hair, but there was no denying it was her. Even at this distance. He blew his whistle to summon the two captains together. She jogged across with the captain's arm band secured around her upper arm.

"Afternoon, ladies", he pipped.

Jessica shook hands with her opponent and stretched an arm towards Gerrard. Their eyes met.

"Gerry. Is that you under that beard?"

He smiled and reached out his hand. "I didn't even know if you were still here. You look well."

The other captain stood in front of them, confused and blurted out "You two know each other then?"

"Yes. We...err...used to be neighbours when we were kids. A long time ago, though."

Gerard immediately reached for the coin in his pocket.

"Heads or tails"

The *Burton Ladies* captain successfully called "Heads" and ran back to change ends. Jessica stood awkwardly next to him trying to think of something meaningful to say.

"It's OK Jess. That was all a long time ago. Let's just get this game started."

With that, he walked over to the centre circle and placed the ball on the spot.

***

The game proved to be both uneventful and without controversy. *Hanley* won with an untidy late goal, deflected in off an opposition defender. As Gerard left the pitch with the players, he looked around for Jess but failed to spot her. She had disappeared into the changing rooms with haste. There would be no opportunity to meet up afterwards. Discuss their time together. After showering and changing he loitered for a while outside the player's changing rooms, but she did not appear. Eventually, Gerard sloped back to his car. It started to rain. He watched the drops of water running down his windscreen and disappearing across the bonnet. A tear began to form in his eye. It summed up more than a thousand words he might have uttered about his melancholic mood.

Crowning glory

The day of days finally arrived. The moment when all those years of preparation and training; honed on endless cold, wet and windy days, officiating between teams that most of the general public had never heard of, were over. On this night he would emerge as a figure of respect in the eyes of the football world. Yes, there would still be ridicule from some, no doubt even within the ranks of players and managers. Despite this, he knew that most of them would recognise the power he now wielded. A controlling influence to affect the outcome of their efforts on the pitch.

A smile began to glow across his face. Gerard stood looking at the mirror in the allocated changing room. He cut a sharp figure, he thought, in his gleaming new referee's kit. Purchased especially for this momentous occasion. He looked at his watch. There was still ten minutes before he was required to knock the dressing room doors to call both teams out. This corner of south London was not the most salubrious place to start his league refereeing career, but he'd been to worse places. Time to calm any pre-match nerves with a visit to the toilet.

A nauseating smell greeted him at the cubicle. A crudely written note was pinned to the outside door:

'WELCOME TO THE FOOTBALL LEAGUE, REF!'

Pushing open the plastic entrance, he stared down at several brown turds in the bowl.

"Oh, for Christ's sake!"

He'd heard about such pranks from other referees. Was this supposed to be a token of endearment? An alternative to a good luck card?

"Professional footballers", he mused, with a shake of the head.

Regardless, he needed to use the facilities and set about cleaning up the mess. It certainly occupied the first part of his waiting time.

Gerard decided to maintain a quiet dignity about the incident. Any over-reaction would surely play into the hands of his tormentors.

"Two minutes, lads!" he shouted through the dressing room doors.

As the players trooped on to the pitch, he made a mental note of two players who could barely hide their smirks.

***

The game began in a downpour. The rain swept across the pitch in diagonal sheets, turning the grass into a brownish-green swamp. The players were doing their best to manage the conditions, moving the ball in wide areas, and bypassing the two quagmires that had developed in both penalty areas. As the game approached the thirty-minute period, the players started to look the same colour as the ground beneath them. It was becoming tricky to identify whether some of the sliding tackles were dangerous play or just challenges that looked worse because the conditions.

Gerard had also become aware of something else. Two of the *United* players bore a striking similarity. In fact, more than just similar. Tall, blond lads, both with mops of hair tied back in ponytails and virtually the same facial features. During a delay for an injury, he spoke to the *City* captain.

"Yes, ref. They're identical twins," but added with a grin, "at least they play at different ends of the field. That should help you tell them apart!"

Gerard looked across at the team in barely visible blue and white. He made a note of the black number nine printed on the back of one of the twin's shirts. The other one was busy berating a team-mate about a mistake that led to the foul on the injured player. His number six on his shirt was only just visible under a blanket of caked mud. He looked in his notebook. It confirmed that one of the twins was booked in the seventeenth minute. The only talking point of a dull first half, bereft of creative play.

An hour in and just when Gerard was starting to relax and enjoy the experience of his first professional match, all hell was let loose.

It started with a sliding tackle that swept the away team's left winger up into the air and crashing into the hoardings, next to the dugout. The guilty player threw his arms up and pointed at the greasy surface. Gerard gave him a critical look and headed towards the crumpled figure on the touchline. He had collided with one of his own coaches and a substitute who couldn't get out of the way. The coach was now on his feet swearing and pointing towards the offender. The victim was still trying to straighten his leg.

Meanwhile, a melee was developing around the other player. Gerard Eymer Pratt recognised the blond hair and ponytail. Number six. Peter Conway. Another yellow card was brandished, followed quickly by the obligatory red one. The same player he had booked in the first half for deliberate hand ball.

Or was it? His number was mostly obscured by the mud. It could have been part of a figure 9. Panic! His brother Ross was also there, provoking an angry reaction from a huddle of visiting players. His number had also largely disappeared from sight.

"It wasn't me ref. It was Ross," the twin shouted confidently. "It was my brother!"

Gerard froze. Had he booked the wrong player? He trotted across to the assistant referee on that side of the pitch. Mr. Cartwright shrugged his shoulders and said he couldn't tell which one of the twins was responsible. "Decisive. Be decisive, Pratt", he mumbled to himself. He could almost feel the cold chill of his assessor's breath encircling his hesitancy.

Four minutes had elapsed since the offending tackle. He called the two captains together.

"I've made a decision" He bellowed. "Number Six is dismissed for two yellow card offences."

"You must be fucking joking, ref. It was me, not my brother who scythed down their winger. You've made a howler here. Give me the yellow card and leave Peter on the pitch."

Gerard Eymer Pratt breathed in deeply and raised his chest to try and look bigger.

"Sorry player. I can't do that. Must go on what I think I saw. And by the way, watch your language or you'll be joining him."

His brother, meanwhile, had moved across to join the discussion. Some of the opposition players were laughing. As Number Six pushed them aside, one of them fell to the ground, holding his face.

"Well you're certainly going off now son," Gerard shouted in exasperation.

The midfield player who hit the ground suddenly got to his feet and stuck his head in Peter Conway's face. Conway stumbled back holding his nose. Pratt had no choice and brandished the red card to the opposition's Number Eight too. Both dismissed players had to be kept apart by their respective coaches and substitutes, as they reluctantly left the pitch.

Then with the game moving towards an increasingly chaotic conclusion, something happened to restore Gerard's belief in the beautiful game. The home striker who hadn't previously produced a single effort on target, suddenly launched himself to meet an in-swinging cross and connected with a scissors-kick that dispatched the ball into the top corner of the net.

"Goal" the locals screamed in unison.

In that moment they forgot Pratt's fumbled attempt to sort out the melee and inwardly rejoiced in a winning goal of stunning quality. Gerard Pratt felt like shaking the goal-scorers hand, but wisely declined. After all, he'd given him the benefit of the doubt after an elbow bloodied his opponent in the first half. Accidental. Maybe. So, should he still have been on the pitch?'

There were further incidents of belligerent behaviour when he blew for full time, with the away team manager and one of the home coaches locking horns in the tunnel. Gerard had almost run out of space in his notebook to record all that had happened. As one of the home players had delightfully put it two hours earlier: "Welcome to the football league, ref!"

A new companion

Just when he had virtually given up the possibility of falling in love again, Gerard met somebody. Or be more accurate, she waylaid him in her hour of need. In somewhat curious circumstances, too. There he was, stood in an under-ground car park in central Birmingham, about to retrieve his car, with darkness descending, when Gerard heard a female voice call out.

"Can anyone help me?"

Somewhere behind a dimly lit blue Vauxhall Corsa, was the outline of women. She stepped out from the car. An elegant young lady dressed in a smart black trouser suit. Clusters of vivid blond hair, cut longer on the left side, obscured one half of her face. She swept the locks back with her hand and stared at the approaching figure. The woman looked agitated. He observed her for several seconds before walking across to introduce himself.

"I'm Gerard," he blurted out almost apologetically. "What seems to be the problem?"

She was crouched down next to one of her rear wheels. The young woman stood up and broke into a smile. Her dilemma needed little explanation. The flat tyre told its own story. "And there's no spare tyre in these vehicles anymore" she continued. The woman pushed her hair back again and cast an engaging glance towards him. "I don't suppose you can help with this thing?"

Gerard already knew there was no spare in her car. He was driving the same model. One year older, maybe and painted metallic grey but nevertheless, the same vehicle. He followed the direction of her eyes before identifying the *thing* that was stoking her angst: the emergency tyre inflator. He didn't need to connect it. Clearly, it had already been used before and was now empty.

"Oh dear." He shared the bad news.

Pratt had had a similar conversation once before. With the garage dealer from which he bought his car. However, in one of his wiser moves during the last twelve months, he'd decided to purchase a spare tyre and wheel on *eBay*. He wasn't convinced with the salesman's pitch that the blow-up tube device would protect him from a serious wheel problem. After all, who wants to drive around, especially on the motorway system, with that kind of risk?

Gerard summoned his most confident face and said he'd be back in a minute. Opening up his boot he emerged with his own spare, rolling it along the concrete floor towards her car.

"This should do the trick." he said.

Gerard used the jack to lift that side of the vehicle and gave the wheel-brace a mighty pull. With a loud cry and a couple of grunts, the damaged wheel was released. She watched, speechless. The new one was swiftly fitted.

"I'm so grateful" she uttered. "My name's Amy, by the way."

What she didn't share with him was the knowledge that her vehicle breakdown cover had expired three months ago.

"I'll certainly get hold of another wheel for you, Gerard. ASAP. I insist!"

"OK. Let me give you my contact details."

He was trying not to stare at her. There was something about this encounter that had made him completely erase memories of that afternoon's INSET on player management. Nothing normally had that impact on him. And it wasn't just testosterone. In her vulnerability he recognised something of his own uncertainty. The referee's training course that day in the second city had suddenly offered an unexpected bonus. A new acquaintance. And who knows?

***

Within a couple of weeks, Amy had secured a replacement wheel. It's subsequent delivery to Gerard's home had led to an offer from him to stay for tea. The offer took her by surprise, but she tentatively agreed. Not for the first time in his life, his crass naivety almost ruined it. His thoughts quickly returned to another meal, several years ago, in a curry house with Jessica.

Learn from your mistakes, you numbly! he whispered to himself. Stop trying so hard to impress!

He was able to offer her pasta with a plate of lightly fried chicken. An indulgent chocolate gateau sat temptingly, on the kitchen table. "Cake always goes down well," he thought, and brought out a bottle of white wine too.

"I hope she's not a vegetarian," he thought, in a panic. "Mm. Should have asked!"

She politely declined the drink. "So, what do you do for a living, Gerard," she asked.

His response left her intrigued. "I've never met a referee before."

"Do you want to come and see me officiate on Saturday?" he exclaimed, rather presumptuously. Her expression confirmed that it didn't constitute the most enticing proposition she'd received that year and Amy made an excuse about a prior engagement.

It wasn't that she hated football. She had grown up with the passions and rituals of sport. Her dad, originally from Scotland, was a *Queens Park Rangers* fan, while her brother had played to a good standard of amateur rugby.

After a couple of persistent e-mail prompts, Amy did agree to meet up for a drink with Gerard, the following weekend. She was attending a meeting, that day, in West London, not far from Gerard's flat. He suggested a pub he knew well and frequented regularly: The *Waggon and Horses*; a choice which had nothing to do with the ambience of the place or the quality of the beer. He was simply well known there.

He'd concluded that there was every chance somebody would recognise him. Tell her how famous he was! It was a nauseatingly devious plan.

On the Saturday evening he wasn't disappointed. She arrived from the hotel event, looking tired and apprehensive. Two guys soon walked past their table and each greeted Gerard with enquiries about where he was refereeing that weekend. Amy cringed. This had to have been choreographed! She looked a little bewildered; even a touch embarrassed, as she was introduced to several members of his personal appreciation society.

With generous grace, she couldn't deny that he'd gone to a lot of effort to make an impression.

"Shall we get something to eat, Amy?"

"As long as you can drag yourself away from your fan base!"

His transparent look required no further explanation.

An hour later, over dinner, she gently challenged him about it. Adopting a more serious demeanour, he abandoned any pathetic babble about coincidences. She glared at him with astonishment.

"I wasn't born yesterday, Gerard."

He grimaced and held his hands up in a gesture of surrender.

"You've read me like a book!"

They both burst out laughing. His idea may not have endeared her to him. But at least she was still there.

***

Gradually, with each passing day, Amy became part of his life. They started to spend more time together. For reasons best known to herself, Amy apparently enjoyed his company. Even when he was talking about football.

She was intrigued by the infectious enthusiasm he displayed for new career; entertained by the conveyor belt of stories he shared with her. The initial banter they demonstrated was developing into something more.

Gerard was not skilled at hiding his emotions. That frantic excitement reserved for couples in the early days of coupling was starting to unfold. Gerard hadn't felt this way for a long time. Not since Jessica.

To his surprise, Amy had grown fond of him too; despite his time-consuming hobby, turned occupation. Although not a football fan herself, she found herself ingratiated into his world of refereeing and began attending some of his matches.

A couple of years younger than Pratt, Amy managed the catering provision for a national company at hotel conferences between the Midlands and London. She had done well in hospitality. A strong-willed and independent woman. She was very different to Jessica. There were none of the belligerence or eye-catching sporting talents. Instead, he had fallen for an independent, conscientious women, with good spirit and endless patience. Gerard's life-long-gift for parading his vulnerability dove-tailed perfectly. Amy seemed happy to cast an emotional blanket around her eccentric boyfriend. He thrived on such attention.

***

In the early stages of their relationship, she had been cautious in sharing details of her own background. Gerard was puzzled that she still lived at home, especially, given her successful career. As the weeks went by, snippets of her past began to surface. She hinted of an un-happy period of her life that had left her traumatised. She eventually confided in him during a weekend away, in Brighton.

Amy had known Grant since their sixth form college days. She was initially flattered by the attentions of this somewhat gangly, handsome youth, who had helped her with their A level

Business Studies assignments. But she soon realised that there was a price attached to his assistance.

One of her friends just told her to be careful. Another girl she knew had gone out with him a few times and confessed to Amy that she was really scared of him. She'd told her that Grant was prone to fits of aggressive and controlling behaviour.

Amy was initially resistant to Grant's attempts to get her out with him on a date. But he had been really helpful to her at college. What's more, she quite fancied him.

Finally, Amy succumbed to the pressure. She agreed to accompany him to a local club. That night the music wasn't to her taste and the volume bombarded her ears, to such an extent that, the only communication possible was physical. Maybe it was deliberate.

Amy wasn't used to being grabbed so unexpectedly and she found his attentions uncomfortable and intrusive. She remembered him squeezing her arm until she winced with pain, in an attempt to kiss her forcibly.

Outside the club there were arguments and more intimidation. Several of his friends looked on as Amy left him there, under a barrage of insults and threats from him. She thought she was making it clear that the evening had been a huge mistake. It wasn't till the Monday morning, when she was back in college, that she realised the full impact of what had happened.

Her friend Rosie bumped into her outside the girl's toilets. "I wouldn't go in there Amy, if I were you."

"What do you mean?"

"You've seriously pissed off somebody, luv!"

She was clutching a scrunched-up poster. A familiar head peered out from the top of the page. Rosie unfurled the rest of the picture. Attached to the body was the heavily sexualised image of some hideous creature, restrained by what looked like large studded belts. These were tied across her breasts and crotch with slogans which declared "Don't touch me. I'm frigid!"

"Is that supposed to be me?" she replied with incredulity.

"Well it's definitely your head!"

Amy looked shocked. Grant Morton's snarling face materialized in her mind. What had she got herself into?

***

It was only the beginning of her ordeal. Messages appeared upon her phone. In college, small groups of giggling students huddled around their face-book pages, titillated by a stream of vulgar comments. Her character was being systematically torn apart. It was all so unfair.

Gerard listened carefully. Some of this resonated with him. His mind returned to his school days and the difficulties he'd endured with his name.

Amy had eventually shared her situation with a college tutor. Grant Morton was summoned to a meeting but claimed it was just light-hearted banter. Nothing was actually proved, but at least it stopped the intimidation.

It left Amy understandably guarded about dating. Her college course was nearing completion. Amy was careful to avoid Grant whenever she caught sight of him around the campus. When their paths did cross, he didn't engage her in conversation. But the glare he delivered instead confirmed that he was far from repentant.

Just when she was starting to regain her confidence, something happened to reignite her fears.

She had started working for a local marketing firm after leaving college. On the way home from work one evening, she was about to walk through her garden gate, when she noticed something moving in the shadows of the old elm trees opposite. Amy stopped to observe the spectre of a man loitering behind the trees. He seemed to be watching her. Tall and wrapped in a long dark coat; his identity further concealed by a black hood pulled down across his face. She moved quickly to the front door and the safety of her family home. Amy sat in the lounge pretending to listen to her mum and sister. She knew her bedroom looked out upon the main street. She tried to distract herself by sharing stories from her day but inside, her mind was racing.

"I'll just freshen up before tea, mum."

Once inside the sanctity of her bedroom, upstairs, she peered, cautiously, through the un-drawn curtains. The elm trees were in full view. And there he was. Still standing there. She was convinced he was now staring up at her.

***

Amy paused for a moment.

"Was it him?" said Gerard.

"Anyway, it all got sorted out." With that she brought the conversation to a close, rather abruptly. "You don't want to hear me rabbiting on anymore," she added.

She stood up and walked out of the room. Amy had shared enough for one day.

It was clear to him that the whole experience had left her with a bitter taste. A couple of weeks later the full details emerged. As she had suspected, the watcher outside her house had indeed been the infamous Grant Morton. However, his attempts to stalk her were swiftly dealt with. Her brother brought an end to Grant Morton's antics in a manner even he could understand.

The Cotterills

Amy decided to introduce Gerard to her family. She was intrigued to see what they would make of him.

"They can be a touch difficult with strangers. Especially my brother, Ian. He's still a little protective," she volunteered, by way of a gentle warning.

That Friday evening she'd arranged for them all to go out together. There was some live music on at the local pub. "Join us."

Gerard Pratt didn't need a second invitation. Despite her comments, he was sure he could cope with big brother. After all, didn't he do that sort of thing for a living; dealing with young, awkward males?

Gerard pulled up outside the large semi-detached house, with its twisted elm tree flanking neat rows of manicured roses. He rang the doorbell to be greeted by the sight of a man mountain. This muscle-bound pillar of rock looked down at the scrawny figure of Gerard Eymer Pratt. "You must be the referee," he said with a critical glance and shouted back. "He's here!"

Amy emerged, dressed in a gloriously seductive top with blue jeans. She looked stunning.

"Go on then, you plonker, introduce yourself."

She wasn't talking to Gerard. Ian thrust his right arm out and grabbed Gerard's hand in a robotic clench, before announcing his name. "Just to let you know I don't like referees. Never have. Especially those involved with the round ball. Nothing personal, mate." And with that, he walked back into the lounge.

"No Problem, my friend," Gerard exclaimed, gingerly, as he rubbed his neck muscles aching from the effort of maintaining eye-contact with Ian.

A female voice interjected. "Don't mind him. My brother can be such a nob!"

He turned around. Stood behind him was an attractive, black-haired woman. Her features carried a strong family resemblance. Amy's younger sister, he guessed, by a couple of years, but similar face and confident mannerisms.

"Hi. I'm Marie. The good-looking member of the family"

"The one with the biggest ego," another voice added. They had been joined by an older woman of about fifty.

"This is Lynn," Marie explained. "Dad's friend."

Her dad, Ross, appeared from the kitchen wearing the image of a naked woman holding up giant vegetables, imprinted across his apron. At least this bizarre spectacle offered a warmer welcome. "Hello there, young man. Not my normal attire" he joked. "Just doing a bit of washing up. Heard a lot about you son. Been looking you up. As far as refs go, you're not that bad."

Almost a compliment, Gerard thought.

Then the lines on his forehead suddenly narrowed. "Apart from that cup match last year, when your ridiculous off-side decision cost *Rangers* the game!" Gerard scratched his head. He couldn't even recall the game he was talking about. He simply smiled and mumbled his apologies.

Introductions complete, Amy's boyfriend was relieved to hear a vehicle's horn sound in the street. It triggered a frantic grabbing of jackets and coats as they all headed out to the waiting taxi. He had survived his initial interrogation relatively intact. Gerard, Amy and Ian, together with Ross, Marie, and Lynn, piled into the vehicle. Lynn turned to Gerard and said how pleased they were that Amy had met someone. His girlfriend made eye-contact and squeezed his hand in acknowledgement.

***

What Gerard hadn't fully realised was that a string of disappointments had followed Amy around the dating network for some time. At the pub, some of these stories began to emerge, fuelled by the alcohol. Their favourite tales always involved Ian. He'd once followed her to check out his sister's date with someone he'd heard was an unsavoury character.

"Yes. A shifty looking guy called Callum" Ian recalled. "He made the mistake of trying to grab her for some un-wanted intimacy."

"Inspector Morse here, staked out the incumbent while he watched from a hidden spot" added Marie.

"Apparently, Ian sprang from the back of a Richmond shop and launched himself at the unsuspecting man. He dragged him in a headlock, down to the Thame's edge. A right hook to his nose sent blood splattering everywhere. He proceeded to duck him in the water for good measure. The shaken male had limped away to lick both his wounded face and his pride.

"Our Ian's a tough bugger," added Mr. Cotterill. Amy doesn't always like him interfering, but you can't argue with that kind of personal security these days."

Amy rolled her eyes and Pratt made a mental note never to kiss Amy if Ian was within half a mile of them!

Gerard soon discovered another reason why Ian didn't seem taken with his sister's new boyfriend. Wrong sport! Her brother was a local rugby player. A real warrior. In fact, he'd played second string for Richmond. A tough, un-compromising back with a short fuse and energy to burn.

Ian did his best to enlighten Gerard.

"The trouble with the round ball game, my friend, is that you guys just don't command enough respect. Too many morons in soccer."

Did he mean the players or the referees?

Ian continued. "I watch TV soccer. None of the players seem to have any discipline. Arguing all the time over throw-ins, off-sides and free-kicks, it's pathetic! I'd send the buggers off for any dissent. No messing! Look at rugby. It's a much harder physical game. Yet the refs have only to raise their hand. Blow the whistle. Everybody stops and responds to the referee."

Do they? Pratt reflected. But he nodded approvingly. He'd made a valid point about lack of discipline.

"Come and watch my team, Gerard. You'd learn a lot!"

Gerard wasn't sure about that either. He would have liked to take issue with some aspects of Ian's management prognosis. But you have to pick your battles carefully in this life, he thought. And Ian didn't sound like a man who was used to being challenged about anything. Especially after he'd already consumed four pints of *Fuller's Pride* that evening.

***

The rest of the evening went as well as it could. The tribute band soon had everyone singing their hearts out and it appeared that the lad from Stoke had made a good impression.

During the next few months his relationship with Amy developed. He was careful to avoid confrontation with members of her family. She seemed to appreciate his patience with Ian and the flirtatious Marie.

One day that following Summer, as they enjoyed a sun-soaked holiday in Greece, he removed a small jewellery box from his jacket and presented her with a ring. "Will you marry me Amy?"

He was not disappointed with the answer. To his joy, Amy threw her arms around him and agreed. The woman he first met with the missing spare wheel had found a space for quirky Gerard in her heart. He didn't know what to say. The shock of receiving her positive answer was almost too much for him.

'El idiota Ingles'

Among all the accolades Gerard had received for his work, the letter that arrived on the mat that Wednesday morning was by far, the most eye-catching.

"Amy. Amy. Come and look at this," he shouted across to his partner, who was busy in the kitchen. "You won't believe what I've been asked to do!"

She appeared, covered in flour. "Take over as England manager?" She quipped, sardonically.

He gave her one of his exasperated looks.

"Go on then. You've got my attention."

He cleared his throat before reading the opening lines.

> *You are invited to officiate as one of our nominated referees, at the forthcoming Europa Under-19 tournament. In Malaga, Spain...*

He quickly scrolled down the page to find the fixtures. There was his name, (at least the part he still used) scrolled against the stand-out fixture: Spain v Portugal. Referee (UK) Gerard E Pratt. Wow! He was also scheduled to run the line in a match between Poland and Germany. Another potentially feisty game. There was an asterisk next to both games, but he had hardly noticed the flagged warnings.

Gerard couldn't believe his luck. Who should he tell first? Well, that honour had already gone to his wife. Amy was now getting excited.

"I hear that Malaga is a lovely city. If work commitments allow, can I come too?"

Gerard couldn't think of anyone he would rather have there to witness his moment of crowning professional glory. An international match.

He browsed through the international briefing document enclosed. A statement from the *Spanish Football Federation* caught his eye. It warned referees of possible tensions between certain neighbouring countries. It cited his first game as a prime example. There was background information about the ongoing political worries concerning the Basque and Catalonia regions, with explanatory notes to help foreign officials to be aware of potential flashpoints.

With the air of a man supremely confident in his abilities, Gerard threw the sheets on the table.

"Mollycoddling, I'd call it." He sighed. "I'm an experienced referee, for heaven's sake! Don't they think I can't deal with a few hot-headed teenagers?"

***

The six weeks wait, simply flew by. Amy had managed to clear her diary and taken leave for the initial qualifying stages of the competition. "Four days of sun, sea and shopping," she said.

If Gerard was lucky enough to be allocated further games, then he was on his own. At that juncture, she would need to fly back to the UK.

The day before the tournament began, they flew into a sunny Malaga. The Pratts checked in to their hotel, which was only ten minutes taxi ride from the stadium. He wondered what sort of attendance such a tournament would attract. Probably not huge, but the Spanish did love their football and the junior international teams had a respected record for showcasing future *La Liga* stars. Many of the young Portuguese footballers taking part were also performing well in the European leagues.

***

Amy sat in the stands as the first game kicked off. Gerard had once again been briefed about what they delicately described as the possibility of 'culturally sensitive' tensions between certain countries and this game was top of the list. Poland were just one of several nations that saw the beating of their opponents, at any level, as a small compensation for the events in Europe during the early 1940s.

Running the line would be an excellent way to initiate him into the world of international youth football. The referee and one of the other linemen were Irish, so there would be no communication challenges, he assumed. He looked around the huge stadium. There were very few people. Just two small noisy groups of partisan supporters, one wielding German, the other Polish flags. They looked for all the world, like extended family outings, boosted by a few friends of the players. The rest of the ground was made up of the coaching teams and some indifferent looking independent locals.

The game was remarkably easy to officiate. Once a couple of early hefty Polish challenges had received the obligatory yellow cards, the game ebbed and flowed. There were plenty of near misses and goals. Noncontroversial goals, the product of sublime skill and shooting power. Easy for a linesman to give confirmative support to his referee. The Poles didn't claim the victory they craved. The Germans won convincingly, 4-1 and Gerard left the pitch looking forward to more of the same in forty-eight hours, when the host nation took on their closest geographical rivals: Portugal.

By coincidence, Gerard and Amy had been on holiday the previous summer in Portugal. A glorious sun-drenched retreat from the pressures of daily life at home. Both had remarked about how similar the culture seemed to be to Spain. And did they love their football! Gerard had watched the likes of past legends like Eusebio and Figo on old videos, not to mention the current goal machine icon that was Cristiano Ronaldo.

Gerard was really looking forward to this new challenge; refereeing the next generation of super stars from two footballing giants.

***

On the day of the game, he was up early. The match didn't kick off till 3.00pm and he was restless. Amy had decided to visit the *Alcazaba Fortress* in the centre of Malaga, that morning, but he didn't really have the time to go with her. An idea came into his head. He thought he'd do a little contemporary research on international rivalries. Gerard walked out of the hotel and looked down the street.

"That looks promising," he thought. He strolled across the road into the local tapas bar opposite and spied a group of elderly men, sat at a table. They seemed to be engrossed in heated discussion, pointing to something in the newspaper which was spread in front of them. He ambled across.

"*Buenos Dias. Habla Ingles?*" (Good morning. Do you speak English?)

One of the men smiled and said "*Si. Un poco, Senor*" (a little)

"*Se puede?*" (May I?)

Gerard pulled up a chair and suggested ordering morning coffee for the table. The others looked at him suspiciously.

The man who responded to him announced himself as 'Paco.' He thanked Gerard for the coffee and asked the Englishman what he wanted to know.

With the aid of Gerard's elementary Spanish and Paco's broken English (which turned out to be rather more impressive), Gerard enquired about the delicate subject of Spanish-Portuguese rivalry. He established that there was normally an edge in sporting events between the nations. He guessed it was far less political than his encounter with the Poles and Germans two days ago, but fascinating, none the less.

Paco summarized the feedback. They saw Portugal as a little brother, (Spain is indeed five times larger) noticeably patriotic, but not beset by the regional divisions that have always plagued Spain. (Basque, Catalan, Andalusian, and the like).

Another man at the table drew his attention to the headlines in the paper. Although he couldn't understand the full meaning, he extracted the words *Catalonia* and *Separardo*. He had absorbed the key point.

Paco reminded Gerard that some of these districts didn't identify closely with Madrid and saw themselves as separate regions. This tension sometimes crossed over into national sporting events, where everybody was expected to respect the national flag.

Gerard had heard enough. He thanked them for their comments and complimented himself on a research activity well managed. The Englishman thought it wise not to reveal why he was interested in the subject. They may have responded a little differently to his probing.

***

Amy was back in good time to join him on the journey at the ground. As they entered the stadium, they could hear the atmosphere building. It was very different to the previous game. There were far more fans in the arena, for a start.

Almost immediately Gerard was approached by a local official with news that one of his linesmen would have to be replaced. He wasn't feeling well. In his place, a tall, wiry looking Frenchman called Jean, had volunteered his services. He caught Gerard outside the official's changing rooms.

"My English is good, so no problem, *Monsieur*."

When Gerard walked out to officiate, he had that same feeling he enjoyed the first time he refereed a league game. He thrust out his chest in pride and gave a wave towards Amy. The usual courtesies about pendant exchanges took place before he shook hands with both captains and took up a dignified stance for the national anthems. How could life get any better than this, he thought?

The Portuguese kicked off and both teams went close to scoring in the opening fifteen minutes. All seemed to be going well until the Spanish conceded a bizarre goal. One of their defenders, under no pressure, inexplicably passed the ball back to where the goalkeeper had been positioned, seconds before. Unfortunately, he'd moved across to the edge of his box and the ball skidded past him into the net. But it was the reaction from some of the other defenders that surprised Gerard. Nobody berated the goalkeeper. Instead, three of his colleagues surrounded the unfortunate culprit who played the ball back to him and there appeared to be some shoving and pushing. Then another reaction. Had he just seen an arm raised in anger against one of their own players? Gerard was shocked. He spoke to his linesmen on radio link to clarify. "It looked like the centre half cuffed him," Jean volunteered.

"What!" Pratt responded. "So much for supporting your teammates!"

The other linesman confirmed a punch had been thrown. Gerard called the suspect over. He was not happy, breaking into an emotional tirade, gesticulating wildly in language Gerard could barely guess. After a deep breath, Gerard brandished a red card. Now the jostling was focussed upon him, as several Spanish players shook their heads and pointed angrily. Nevertheless, the decision had been made and he held his ground until the players retreated to their own half to re-group.

The crowd seemed to foam at the mouth and cried for justice. Their attention turned to the referee. "El referee es bastardo!" some cried. He understood perfectly but tried to remain focused.

Every time the Spanish fullback who had unfortunately scored the opening goal, received the ball, there were boos and angry words.

Meanwhile, the Portuguese players looked bewildered. They hadn't played particularly well, but with the defiance of their own goalkeeper and the opposition's help, they found themselves a goal up and facing ten men.

Gerard was pleased to blow the half-time whistle and rushed to the sanctuary of the official's room.

"What was all that about guys?"

Jean and Peter, his English assistant, shared their thoughts with him. "Looks to be some sort of political reaction. *Garcia,* their number two, is a Basque player. No love lost with some of the others, I'm afraid," Peter suggested.

"We'll have to keep a close eye on this, lads," Gerard stated. "The second half could be lively." He finished his tea and clenched his fists. "I'm in charge of this game and nothing is going to threaten my fair handling of what happens on the pitch."

The Spanish team had clearly had a serious talking to at half time and came out bursting at the seams. After ten minutes of constant pressure, the Spanish won another corner. The ball was crossed, tantalisingly, into the penalty area, where the debutant number ten stretched his leg and hooked the ball into the net. A volcanic eruption of noise reverberated around the stadium. With some relief, Pratt awarded the goal and pointed to the centre circle. But the crowd had seen something to vent their spleen. The goal scorer had removed a small Catalan flag from his pocket and was racing around the pitch holding it for all to see. Suddenly, two spectators had appeared on the pitch and were heading towards the Catalonian nationalist. Jean managed to intercept the first, but the second collided with the scorer and knocked him to the ground. Many in the crowd chanted '*Ole!*' By the time Gerard and the stewards had got to him, the young striker had been pole-axed. He lay on the ground, while the stretcher was summoned. Clearly still dazed, the young man was substituted, to rousing cheers from the spectators.

The replacement player was warmly welcomed to the pitch. He was a young hopeful from Real Madrid and the message was obvious. A local, a Spaniard from the capital and a patriot!

Gerard sensed the fans were increasingly seeing him as the villain of the drama. He disallowed a brilliant scissors-kick from the newly arrived *Sanchez* (correctly, according to the linesman) and let some pretty robust challenges on other Spanish players go unpunished.

Another chant echoed around the ground. *"El referee es un idiota."*

But two minutes from the end, a breath-taking move, straight from an unsuccessful Spanish corner, sent the Portuguese playmaker right through the centre of Spain's defence to round the keeper and fire home. Although he had little to do with it, Gerard became aware of a growing chant around the ground *"El arbitrar es un idiota."*

He spoke to his linesmen. "What does *arbitrar* mean, guys?"

Peter said "Not sure, Gerard, but idiota means idiot."

Jean said "I'm afraid *arbitrar* also means referee, my friend. Just ignore it."

The microphone went silent as Gerard contemplated what most of the ten thousand bodies in the ground were chanting. Now he was angry. *It wasn't his bloody fault that half the Spanish team couldn't stand each other, and the other half couldn't stop the counterattack that won the game!* he grimaced.

It was the last significant incident of the match. That is, if he chose to ignore the cascade of empty water bottles and odd pieces of fruit that rained down on Pratt, as he entered the tunnel. He made a note in his book. Painful as this experience was, it was not as bad as the excruciating sight of two suited representatives from the FA walking past him; casting disapproving glances towards Gerard, without saying so much as a word.

***

Later that evening, Gerard sat at the restaurant with Amy, consuming his third glass of *San Miguel*. They watched the sun soaking the skyline bright red, as the light started to fade.

"Well I guess it didn't go as well as I hoped, after all, did it?" he pronounced, with an excruciating gift for stating the obvious. "A bit harsh, though, not being selected to officiate at the knock-out stage, don't you think?"

Amy just looked at him. It required no further amplification.

"But things can always be worse," he added, with a touch of sanguine hindsight.

The coming months would prove how right he was.

All good things....

"Traumatic moments in life can sometimes emerge from the most innocuous of events, my love."

That's what Amy told him when it happened.

It provided little comfort to her husband. Gerard Eymer Pratt had reached the pinnacle of his ambition. A football league referee, with all the publicity and attention that the role created. There was now much more local recognition from his TV appearances. Money from officiating at high profile games. In fact, more money than his modest Housing Department career had ever provided. Gerard had abandoned his work in the Local Authority the moment his professional contract had arrived. There were now more opportunities for travel, as his professional skills took him to work at tournaments in other parts of Europe.

Although he dreamed of fixtures at Barcelona and Madrid, there was a sense of realism about this. He wasn't going to oust that bank of highly experienced refs who secured such games. Nevertheless, he was content with occasional trips to France or Belgium to officiate at European under 17, 19 and 23 games. His less than auspicious performance in Malaga had not stopped these opportunities completely, just limited them.

The *Football Association* had reviewed his performance and concluded that he had been a touch unfortunate.

Meanwhile, Amy continued to get time off her own working commitments to join him at matches. Making a weekend of it. He loved that.

The only blot on the perfect life he now enjoyed was the absence of *little feet*. They had tried to have children, but it hadn't happened. Amy had the usual fertility challenges associated with a woman in her late thirties, while tests also revealed that Gerard had a low sperm count. But they had resigned themselves to the situation and with their new lifestyle, hadn't considered other alternatives to starting a family.

Then it happened. And it wasn't a pregnancy!

Gerard was refereeing a premier league game at the end of the season on Tyneside, between Newcastle and Brighton. Both teams were staring at the possibility of relegation and the atmosphere was tense. Tackles from each side flew into their opponents with the desperation of fear. The ball was pumped from one penalty area to the other with directness more associated with lower league matches.

With both sides favouring such long-ball tactics, keeping up with the play was proving to be a nightmare. Even for a fit lad like himself.

Pratt scurried up and down the pitch like a panther; devouring and adjudicating each challenge with the frenzy of a wild cat. Suddenly, he felt a twinge, then a snapping sound from the back of his right leg and a sharp pain in his hamstring, forced him to the ground. The physio who came on to the pitch shook his head and cast a sympathetic glance in his direction.

Gerard had not been substituted since his days as a rarely used six-a-side player, nearly twenty years before. His assistant referees helped him off the pitch, amidst the usual chorus of laughter from the crowd. He'd never understood why some of the spectators found an injury to the referee so amusing. In the past, when he was playing, any substitution he experienced was normally taken because he was playing so badly! Now, racked with pain, he could only curse his bad luck.

Amy had not been present at the game. She was busy organising a corporate event in Burton-On-Trent. He was initially more embarrassed than anything else when he rang her. At least he hadn't driven up to the North-East, so his car was at home. The medical staff at Newcastle patched him up with an ice pack and a tight bandage and told him to rest the leg as soon as he got home. As he hobbled to the taxi, Gerard was already working out in his head how many fixtures he might miss because of the injury. Two to three months, the physio had guessed.

Amy was there to meet him at the station in London. It was quiet, at that time of night and he hobbled along the platform until they spotted a lift. Forty minutes later he pushed open the front door of his house in Ealing and collapsed onto the sofa. The effect of the painkillers was now wearing off. He asked his wife to pour him a large brandy.

There were several good-will messages on his *twitter* feed. Bob and Steve, fellow referees he got on well with, had heard. Together with an official from the Referees Association and one of the Newcastle players. He ignored a couple of others which offered less supportive comments about his leg dropping off and one lamenting the fact that it wasn't his head! Finally, a home fan had restored his mood by wishing him all the best for his recovery.

But he didn't recover. Despite receiving extensive physio, the hamstring remained very sore. The FA sent him for a scan. His wife drove him to the private hospital, barely five miles from their home. Extensive damage to the thigh was identified. 'A grade three tear,' the doctor declared. He inspected the bruising which extended right up to his buttocks. Gerard told him it made him wince when he clenched them.

"Well stop clenching them!" Amy advised helpfully.

"You've picked up a bad one here, my friend," the specialist announced.

"It's going to be a minimum of three months."

"But I keep myself really fit," Pratt pleaded, as if that could mitigate against the seriousness of the injury.

"That might be part of the problem, Gerard. I've treated hundreds of sportsmen and women for similar injuries. You're going to have to be patient with this one."

Gerard looked at him incredulously. Patience may have been one of Gerard's strongest assets, but after all that training.

Really? He thought about all those long jogs, regardless of the weather. He had pushed himself, mercilessly, to ensure that he could keep up with the play; regardless of how quick some of the players were. It gave him an edge, he thought. But at what cost, now?

Ten weeks elapsed. The bruising gradually subsided and the physiotherapy exercises were painstakingly practiced. He still needed to rest the leg regularly and struggled to sleep at night. Now spending large parts of his days on the sofa, Gerard's waistline was beginning to expand. He pinched the flesh around his hips. For a moment he panicked.

"God, I'm turning into my dad!"

He shuddered at the thought.

Scattered around the lounge was his collection of footballing memorabilia. Souvenirs of a lifetime's devotion to the sport he loved. Over the weeks, Gerard had exhausted every football video in his extensive collection. His set of soccer autobiographies were well thumbed. He was now reading Graham Poll's book 'Red Card' for a third time and for the first time since he began officiating, he was really bored.

The days dragged on as he limped across to the car and drove to the park for a change of scenery. With the aid of a crutch Pratt went shopping, even when he didn't want to buy anything. He drove across to a local amateur team to watch them training. Amy was often out all day and he found the silence of the house a frustrating place to be.

Eventually, things started to get better. The pain occurred less frequently, and his mobility improved. "Be careful not to over-stretch the hamstring too much," the specialist had said.

But Gerard was a man in a hurry. The life he'd loved; built up from such meagre beginnings, was falling apart and he needed to get back as soon as possible. He started walking in boots around the local park and graduated to light jogging. Amy kept telling him to slow down.

"You've waited so long to improve, Gerard, don't do too much too soon."

Gerard nodded but wasn't listening. In his head, all he could visualise was him striding out at one of the countries' finest stadiums, ready to keep all those household names in order. Just a few weeks more and he'd be ready.

***

Colleagues from the Referee's Association were pleased to see Pratt.

"So, you're ready to return, Gerard. Good stuff! Let's get you up to speed with a couple of lower league matches before plunging you back into the higher-level stuff, ah?"

Gerard looked disheartened.

"Don't look so glum son. I'm sure you'll soon be back at the top table. You've always been such a whippet racing around the pitch."

As every runner knows, there's a world of difference between jogging gently and running at full pelt. Pratt was shortly going to be reminded of this reality in the worst possible scenario. In front of paying customers!

Game set and match!

His comeback game featured a trip to a club where he hadn't worked before. *Wycombe Wanderers'* Adam's Park ground. He looked at the league table. They were riding high in third spot. Their opponents *Forest Green Rovers* were at the opposite end of the table. A side trying to establish itself in the league after many years operating in non-league football. He perused the match statistics of both teams to glimpse something about their approach to playing. *Wycombe,* unsurprisingly for a team near the top had an excellent disciplinary record. Not a single red card, a sprinkling of yellows and no suspensions. Peering across at *Forest Green's* statistics, they also seemed to be a fairly clean outfit. They had lost one player to an automatic red and subsequent suspension, but appeared to be a good football team, scoring freely. Their Achilles heel was the defence. Forty-seven goals conceded from twenty-four games already and it was only January. It certainly looked like it could be a high scoring game.

But what about the conditions? It had been raining for most of the week and the pitch looked more like a swamp. Gerard guessed the game would still go ahead but he would do his usual checks.

As he made his way to the ground that morning the rain stopped, and the sun made a brief appearance. But his walk across the pitch confirmed his fears. There were pools of standing water around the centre circle and pits of mud forming in both penalty areas. He tested the run of the ball. Not much flow in these areas but running free on the grassy wide sections. Just enough to play the match, he deduced, but his mind was also deliberating about his personal challenge. The hamstring would only take a certain amount of stretching in such conditions. All that twisting and turning in the mud. He'd have to be careful. After all, he hadn't been totally honest with either the FA or his wife about the injury. There were still twinges. Even so, Gerard was desperate to give it a try.

Despite the mud and a forecast of more rain, Gerard passed the game fit to play. He disappeared for a pre-match bite to eat in the hospitality area, bumping into one of the longest serving managers in the league. "Just a light lunch," he joked with him, to provide some much-needed fuel for his exertions. The clouds were gathering again by the time he trotted out with the teams. The fresh November air filled Gerard Pratts' lungs with expectation. He was back! What he hoped for was a more measured passing game between these teams, with less running for him. What he didn't need was the ball being punted from one goalkeeper to another. The conditions certainly encouraged such tactics and mistakes would be made. But Gerard needed to pace himself. He was already feeling his hamstring. After a rather cagey twenty-five minutes, the *Forrest Green* keeper sent an enormous kick down the length of the field. The centre-half jumped and missed it. He seemed to have been impeded. Curtis, the away team's number nine, drew the goalie and thumped the ball past him into the net.

Gerard watched from a distance. He was still labouring to reach the half-way line, let alone see how the move had led to a goal on the edge of the penalty area. *Wycombe* players surrounded him, indicating that Curtis had blatantly elbowed their number five out of the way before scoring. Surely, he had seen it.

Gerard consulted his linesman. Neither of them was sure but his assistant thought there was contact. There were, however, lots of bodies obstructing their view. Decision time, he thought. With a deep breath he shouted, "Its' a goal" and pointed to the centre-circle. One of the home coaches, incensed by the decision, sprinted from his technical area and made a beeline towards him.

"Come on ref. you must be joking. How can you give that? You were still in your own half!"

He didn't need reminding of his limited view of the incident.

"Sorry, pal. I didn't see any foul play. The goal stands. And you need to return to your technical area."

"Well fuck you, ref!"

Pratt was shocked. He wasn't used to being verbally abused like this, by coaches. He had no choice. He reached for the red card in his back pocket and brandished it towards the agitated coach of the away team.

"Foul and abusive language. I've no option but to send you to the stands."

His assistant manager grabbed him by the arm and pushed him away from Gerard. Meanwhile, a group of players were pushing and shoving each other in the centre of the field. As he ran across to them with haste, he felt the pain. His hamstring was telling him to stop running. He hobbled the remaining distance and succeeded in calming them down. The hosts finally kicked off and the game continued.

Gerard grimaced. He had a volatile situation to manage and only one good leg to get him there.

Everywhere he looked there was mounting tension. *Wycombe's* coaching team were gesticulating angrily at the away bench. The fourth official had already communicated to him via radio link that conflict was brewing. Certain players continued to goad each other, while the home supporters were vociferously baying for his blood.

One of the linesmen franticly waved his flag to attract his attention. An item had been thrown onto the pitch. It looked like a cigarette lighter. Gerard made a note in his pad and waved play on.

The home side were now camped outside their opponent's penalty area, trying to force an equalizer. Shots were pinned into the massed line of bodies protecting their goal. They bounced off defenders, including one that was only just hacked off the line. Then a rocket of a shot flew past the keeper and crashed against the crossbar. It rebounded down over the goal-line. At least, he thought it had. The linesman wasn't so sure and nor was Pratt.

"Goal!" shouted the *Wycombe* fans in unison. Their players hugged the goal-scorer in delirious celebration.

Once again Pratt had an important call to make. But he just wasn't sure it had crossed the line.

"No goal," he eventually shouted, much to the delight of the away fans.

The home players surrounded him and gesticulated angrily. "It was over the line ref. Everybody saw it!"

Gerard Eymer Pratt limped back to the centre circle. Two decisions. Two goals. Both had gone against the home team. And one of their coaches sent to the stands. All this and it wasn't even half time! His leg was really starting to stiffen up as the forty-five minutes finally elapsed. At least half time would give him the opportunity to get some treatment on it.

He could appreciate their frustrations as an infamous chant broke out amongst the Wycombe supporters:

"You don't know what you're doing!"

Followed by:

*"Who's the w****r in the black,*
*Who's the w****r in the black.*
Eymer Pratt, Eymer Pratt.
*He's the w****r in the black."*

It had been a while since he heard those lines. Gerard was escorted from the pitch by his assistant referees and linesmen, to choruses of boos and more unsavoury chants. He sought medical help from one of the physios, although he wisely chose to seek out one from the visitor's changing room.

As the physio strapped his left thigh up, both assistant referees appeared to check on the condition of their team leader.

Gerard shared his anxieties about the leg with them. "Thanks for your support guys. I'm going to try to keep going, but if I can't continue are you all right Bob, to take over?"

Bob nodded. He couldn't believe Gerard was even contemplating the second half.

"Given all that's happened and the conditions, I'll say one thing for you *Pratt*. You've got guts!"

But courage alone was not going to drag him through another forty-five minutes of frantic football. The boos erupted again as Gerard hobbled out to begin the second half. He'd decided to position himself no more than three metres either side of the centre-circle, to minimise the running (or rather, shuffling) he would need to do to see the play. He was going to rely on the guys running the line to flag any offence too far away. His assessor, sat in the stands, would not have been impressed. He needed to come off and let somebody else referee the remainder of the game.

Fifteen minutes later, and with Gerard in agony, the *Wycombe* number seven raced on to a flicked pass. As he turned to shoot, he appeared to stumble and clip his own leg. Down he went in a heap.

"Penalty," the crowd screamed. Gerard did something he'd rarely done in his career with penalty claims. He panicked.

Maybe he was conscious of the balance of his key decisions in the first half. Maybe he was persuaded by the pleas of the home players, but he pointed to the spot. Immediately he was surrounded by a posse of visiting shirts, while their small band of fans chanted "Cheat! Cheat!"

The nearest linesman to the incident cast an incredulous glance in his direction and through his microphone told him bluntly: "I think you've got that one wrong, Gerry. I reckon he accidently tripped himself over."

"From where I'm looking Bob, I think the defender caught him. Going to have to give it."

When everybody had calmed down, the spot kick was dispatched with venom past the visiting keeper. 1-1. Half an hour to go. Game On!

But not for Gerard Pratt. It proved to be his parting gift to the drama as he collapsed onto the pitch, holding his thigh.

"Penalty!" the away fans shouted in mock derision. Even some of the players broke into smiles.

It's a special talent that enables an official to upset both sets of supporters in equal measure, but that was Gerard's legacy this day.

As Pratt was helped from the pitch by the home team's medical team, little did he realise the significance of the moment.

As Bob Simpson took over from him, the referee's match assessor was still scrawling furiously in his notebook.

"Not the most edifying of comebacks."

Humble pie

Gerard had torn his hamstring again. The same one. This time there was little sympathy. The damage was self-inflicted, and it was serious. There was a long queue of individuals waiting to find out what exactly had happened.

Amy had been absent from the game. She had not been convinced about the idea that he was ready to return. All those endless discussions and warnings. She was right. As she collected him from the hospital that evening, there was frustration and anger in her voice.

"I told you, didn't I. You're just so stubborn. Now look at you. Back to square one."

His specialist at the hospital raised an eyebrow and exclaimed that they were into new territory now. His prognosis was not encouraging. "Back to square one would be an optimistic prediction."

If things weren't bad enough, the referee's assessor submitted a damning indictment of his performance on the day.

> *In the sixty minutes Gerard Pratt officiated, he made several serious errors of judgement, leading to the award of goals that should not have been given. He was physically unable to keep up with the play. There was also evidence of a bewildering disregard for his assistant referee's opinions, when he was better placed to see specific incidents. It culminated in the bizarre award of a penalty kick to a player who clearly fell over his own legs.*

Most humiliating of all was the final comment.

> *Mr. Pratt's general decision making and inability to stamp any authority on proceedings, led to a volatile atmosphere in the ground that was not conducive to the spirit of the game.*

Gerard read the report in a state of some despair. In all the years he had officiated at games he'd never received such negative feedback. Hadn't they understood what he was dealing with? Were there no allowances for his injury?

The report carried another letter from the FA. It seems there had been a lot of media coverage of his performance and questions were being asked of the Association itself. Both teams had submitted critical comments about how the match was officiated. How had he been allowed to referee the game when he was clearly physically unfit?

Gerard was required to attend an informal hearing to explore some of this further.

***

Two weeks later he sat before the disciplinary committee and did his best to defend his actions on the day. In his defence, Gerard had previously been considered to be something of a rising star. Furthermore, his previous assessments had been encouraging.

It was decided that this was probably just an unusually bad day, brought on by his desire to get back on the pitch too soon after a long injury. Nevertheless, he must recognise that the game was not about individuals. He clearly wasn't ready to return that day and showed poor judgement in thinking he was. In future, he would be required to show clear medical evidence that he was fit to resume his duties.

Meanwhile, during his extended absence, he was instructed to attend all the training events outlined in the *Referees Association* website. This would begin with the forthcoming Thursday seminar on the use of enhanced technology to assist the referee. It would include something being trialled in parts of Europe and America called VAR. Gerard looked puzzled.

"It means *Video Assisted Referee*, a member of the panel announced. It's coming our way soon and we need to be ready to trial it."

Gerard tried to look interested and agree to their demands. He had little choice.

"One last thing, Mr. Pratt. In no circumstances should you talk to the press. They're just itching to make a *mountain out of* a *molehill* with this one."

Within five minutes, he had hobbled back into the waiting area.

"At least they haven't sacked me!" he mused.

A vision from a VAR

As his train pulled into the National Exhibition Centre station, in Birmingham, several people he recognised stood up to get off. There were cursory glances from faces he recognised and a couple of enquiries about his injury. Gerard's story had made it to the back pages of the tabloids, thanks to the perseverance of a particularly tenacious journalist. Although some of his refereeing colleagues had been critical of his decision-making in his game at Newcastle, there was some sympathy amongst them for his efforts to get fit for the game. But there was no denying the seriousness of what had unfolded. The sports journalist had unearthed several issues about the pressures facing modern referees and his story had ruffled the feathers of the *Football Association*. As far as the injury was concerned, his thigh was still heavily strapped, and the crutches had re-appeared. John, one of his refereeing pals on the circuit, had spotted him and called across.

"Need some help there, Gerry?"

He certainly did, as he tentatively disembarked from the train. Once out of the carriage, he sat on a platform bench, waiting for a disabled buggy. John kept him company as they caught up on recent news. He had already spoken to Gerard on the phone and had discussed the outcome of the disciplinary panel.

"It all sounds a little harsh, my friend. We all have bad days in this job. Guess you're going to be out now for some time?"

Gerard gave him a despondent nod. "What do you know about VAR then?" He was keen to move the discussion away from his enforced sabbatical. "According to what I've been reading, it's only a couple of years away from all the top leagues of European football, including here?"

John had a refereeing mate in America who had been using it all year. "It's not without its controversies, he reckons.

Sometimes it takes an eternity for a decision to be checked and some of the off-side decisions are still debatable."

The arrival of the buggy was a necessary distraction. Gerard was already harbouring doubts about this latest technological gadget to help referees.

The auditorium was unusually full. It was clearly a topic that had aroused interest amongst officials around the country. A series of presentations unfolded for their deliberation. VAR was presented as a major step forward in eliminating human error. A panacea to deal with those difficult moments when match officials were not too certain what had actually taken place. They ploughed through reams of video footage, mainly from the United States, to show how the technology had dealt with specific issues. Marginal off-sides, illegal penalty area tackles, and hand-ball appeals were slowed down, repeated, to ensure the referee could check, or rather, an off-pitch panel could check, what the decision should be.

Extensive discussion took place in the room. There were clearly concerns, especially about the number of stoppages that would occur and the length of time it would take for agreement to be reached. Some in the room were not convinced.

"Football has always been a game of quick changing dramas, requiring quick decisions," said one.

"All these stoppages will just kill the atmosphere in the stadiums. What's so wrong about the current system?" said another.

"It's driven the game forward for over a hundred years. Referees have never been better trained, fitter or more skilled in their professional reactions?" shouted a third voice in the audience.

There was plenty of vocal support for these views. The presenters did their best to pacify the dissenters. They introduced their ace card. It was a series of film clips of important goals, either wrongly disallowed or others, chalked off, that should have stood. Surely, they argued, the supporters want to see justice done. VAR could ensure that these key decisions would be made correctly.

"But at what cost?" some complained.

"Are we going to see matches running into fifteen minutes of additional time?" There was some laughter in the audience. Others reflected that they already had radio contact with each other, and this innovation was supposed to have reduced the number of referee mistakes during matches. Had it not?

Gerard listened throughout, with a sense of despondency. From where he sat, there seemed to be a hidden agenda in all this. All that human interaction between players and referees was in danger of vanishing as the robotic presence of VAR took up ultimate responsibility for match legislation. He was sure the TV studios would articulate each incident in all its mathematical wonder. Lines would be drawn. Players' fingers and toes would be deemed to be 'just' off-side, and everyone would congratulate themselves on the minute accuracy of the process.

But what about the fans? The spirit of the game? How were they to react to all this? Would they eventually get bored with these constant interruptions and abandon the game? And what about the referee? How much extra pressure was all this going to put them under. Him under?

He left the conference with a heavy heart. All the joys associated with refereeing; the reasons he had entered the profession in the first place, that challenge to stand up and be the central figure of authority, was going to change. A computer would adjudicate, what had previously been his territory. He wasn't sure that this was the sort of refereeing he wanted to do. It may have been a little way off, but it was going to be used in the next World Cup. The writing was on the wall.

***

The neon signs of Highbridge hospital lit up against an ashen sky, as Amy drove him into the carpark. He wasn't sure what the doctors would say. Despite the rest, there remained constant pain in his hamstring area and it didn't seem to be getting any better. Further examination confirmed his worst fears: there were complications. The body was not restoring full movement to the connecting muscles and the tissue area was not healing properly.

A sullen faced specialist spelled out his diagnosis.

"The bad news, I'm afraid, is that you may have to accept some restricted movement from this part of your body in the future."

Gerard's jaw dropped as the full weight of the report hit him, head on.

"Do you mean I won't be able to run freely?"

"You may not be able to *run* at all, I'm afraid."

Amy grabbed his hand, but the gesture provided little comfort.

"You know what I do for a living, doctor. Don't you?"

"Yes, I do. I understand how hard this must be."

***

Gerard sat in his favourite chair, looking out through the open door of his porch. The luscious lawn twinkled in the sunshine as each blade shook off the last semblance of yesterday's rain. A pigeon forsook its foraging to turn and stare at him.

He thought about the countless green spaces he had run across in pursuit of a football dream. Not for him the adoration of fans nor the admiration of other players. Just to stand on the same hallowed pitches was everything for a boy who couldn't even make the school soccer team. The memories came flooding back; Mr. Becket, Kevin, Phil, Sean and Raj. Jessica, Mr. Brough, Bob and Mat Jones. Rafael. Through endurance, determination and a willingness to survive, his dream had been fulfilled. But all good things come to an end and the news from the hospital confirmed as much.

"What will you do now?" Amy asked. "We both know that this is going to leave a huge hole in your life."

"I've got a healthy pension, and the love of a good woman. I think we'll survive."

"Well, I will but I'm not sure about you!" she joked. "I hope you're not intending to spend the next stage of your life sitting around watching TV football all day?"

Gerard broke into a grin. "Funny you mention that because I've had an idea..."

THE END

ACKNOWLEDGEMENTS

My thanks to Sue Gazey for her editorial scrutiny of the story; Mike Iland, for his background insights on the training of referees, and the Oldswinford Writers for their continuous support in the construction of this narrative.

FICTION FROM APS BOOKS
(www.andrewsparke.com)

AJ Woolfenden: *Mystique: A Bitten Past*
Davey J Ashfield: *Footsteps On The Teign*
Davey J Ashfield *Contracting With The Devil*
Davey J Ashfield: *A Turkey And One More Easter Egg*
Fenella Bass: *Hornbeams*
HR Beasley: *Nothing Left To Hide*
Lee Benson: *So You Want To Own An Art Gallery*
Lee Benson: *Where's Your Art gallery Now?*
Lee Benson: *Now You're The Artist...Deal With It*
Lee Benson: *No Naked Walls*
TF Byrne *Damage Limitation*
Nargis Darby: *A Different Shade Of Love*
J.W.Darcy: *Ladybird Ladybird*
Jean Harvey: *Pandemic*
Michel Henri: *Mister Penny Whistle*
Michel Henri: *The Death Of The Duchess Of Grasmere*
Michel Henri: *Abducted By Faerie*
Amber J Hughes: *An Injection Of The Unexpected*
Hugh Lupus *An Extra Knot*
Ian Meacheam: *An Inspector Called*
Tony Rowland: *Traitor Lodger German Spy*
Andrew Sparke: *Abuse Cocaine & Soft Furnishings*
Andrew Sparke: *Copper Trance & Motorways*
Phil Thompson: *Momentary Lapses In Concentration*
Paul C. Walsh: *A Place Between The Mountains*
Paul C. Walsh: *Hallowed Turf*
Michael White: *Life Unfinished*

Printed in Poland
by Amazon Fulfillment
Poland Sp. z o.o., Wrocław

54278780R00060